Perfect Disaster.

The third novel in the Perfect Series.

Written by

Lindsey Powell.

A CIP record of this book is available from the

British Library.

The Perfect Series

Perfect Stranger

Perfect Memories

Perfect Disaster

To all of you who have supported me so far,

Get ready to continue the perfect journey.....

Chapter One.

Stacey.

I stand, with my arms folded across my chest, and I survey my surroundings. I watch as people all around me are enjoying themselves, drinking and dancing to the music. Most of them are unwinding after a long week at work. I smile as Susie catches my eye. She is busy behind the bar, serving drinks to a rowdy hen party. As I look around, I can see that all of my hard work has paid off. My eyes wander to the dance floor and I see Lydia and Martin bopping away to the nineties dance music. Tonight, I stand here, as the new manager of The Den. I have had complete control of the refurbishment that I have been working hard on, all week long. Now that this place is under new management, I thought that it would be good to put my own stamp on the place. I had various workers in here early in the mornings, who then worked late into the night, so that the place was ready for tonight, the opening night. Being able to manage this place has brought out a drive in me that I didn't expect at all. I have actually quite enjoyed myself, even if it has been a little stressful at times. The Den's makeover has given the place more of a modern feel. The walls are now black and white monochrome, and the sleek new furnishings have helped to give a sexy but hip vibe. The black enamelled tables and chairs look great in contrast to the grey flooring. The dance floor has been made up of black and white squares, which has added a retro aspect. Lydia and Martin thought that the place looked fantastic. The energy filling this room tonight is infectious, but I can't fully absorb it as there is something missing. Actually, what I should say is, there is someone missing. Jake. He had to go away on a business trip a week ago, meaning that he hasn't been able to make the opening tonight. He actually went the day after I moved in with him. *Talk about shitty timing.* What makes it even worse is that I have only spoken to him a couple of times since he has been gone. We keep missing each other's calls. Either he has been in meetings or I have been busy getting this place ready. I have no idea when he is due back either. Apparently, the deal that he is trying to negotiate is taking much longer than expected. I miss him like crazy. It doesn't feel right for him to not be here. I sigh and blow a lock of my hair out of my eye. I see Martin making his way towards me and I force a smile.

"Baby girl, this place is banging. You have done a fabulous job."

"Thanks Mart," I say, mustering up as much cheeriness as I can.

"Why the sad eyes? I thought that you would be pleased with the number of people that have turned out tonight to see the place?"

"I am pleased," I reply. "I just miss Jake, that's all," I say with a sigh.

"Ahhhh, look at you. I never thought that I would see the day when you became a love-sick puppy," Martin teases.

"Fuck off," I retort.

"Oooooh, bitchy." It's a good job that Martin and I understand each other's sense of humour. He knows that I am only playing with him.

"Want some more champagne?" I ask as I make my way behind the bar before Martin can answer. He is bound to say yes so I don't know why I bothered to ask in the first place. I take a bottle of the finest champagne from the fridge and return to Martin, who is now sat on one of the bar stools. I grab two glasses from behind the bar and place them in front of us.

"Is it on the house?" Martin asks me.

"Yes Mart, it's on the house." I pop the cork and pour us each a glass.

"I knew that there was a reason why I became friends with you," he says, winking at me. I poke my tongue out at him and he starts to laugh. We clink our glasses together and I take my first sip. This is the first drink that I have allowed myself so far tonight. I didn't want to drink alcohol too early on as I know that I am here until closing time. I moan quietly in appreciation as the bubbles slide down my throat. I spot Paul weaving his way through the crowd, heading towards Martin and I. I grab another champagne glass and by the time he has reached us, I have poured his drink and am holding the glass out to him.

"Thanks Stace," he says as he takes the glass, sits down on a bar stool next to Martin, and takes a big gulp of his drink. "That's some good shit," he comments, taking a sip this time.

"Ah, a man who appreciates the finer things in life," Martin says as he turns to Paul. Martin is always flirting with Paul. Paul doesn't seem to mind though. In fact, the two of them are forming quite a bromance.

"Hey Paul?" I cut in before they start a full-blown conversation about whatever random topic they decide to debate today. "Have you heard from Jake today at all?"

"Nah. He's busting his balls to close whatever deal it is that he has gone to negotiate. I guess he's too busy to bother with us little people right now." Paul laughs, clearly cracking a joke, but I flinch a little at his words. He quickly sees that I am not amused and abruptly halts his laughter. "Oh god, I was only joking Stace," he says, looking panicked.

"I know, I guess I'm just a little sensitive at the moment," I reply, trying to brush off my reaction to his comment.

"Have *you* not heard from him then?" he asks, looking a little shocked at having to ask me this question.

"I had a text from him this morning to wish me good luck for tonight. Apart from that though, I haven't heard a thing from him."

"Oh Stace, you know that he wouldn't miss tonight if this deal wasn't really important." I know that what Paul is saying is the truth, but I still feel disappointed that he isn't here.

"I know, I know," I say, dismissively. I really did think that he would have been back by now though. It better be a great fucking deal that he is negotiating. "It just doesn't feel right with him not being here. I miss him."

"Oh baby girl," Martin chimes in. "He's the one who is missing out tonight. I mean, look at you. Talk about rocking the sexy boss lady vibe. You got it going on." I frown as I look down to my clothes. I have no idea what Martin is talking about. I picked the simplest outfit for tonight, consisting of black, leather trousers, a black sleeveless shirt that is tucked into the front of my trousers with the back hanging down loose and dark grey shoe boots. I raise my eyebrows at Martin. He must be more pissed than I thought.

"You're clearly more pissed than I realised," I say to Martin as I voice my opinion out loud.

"Seriously, you are one hell of a hot boss and you don't even realise it. That makes the vibe that you are giving off even more sexy."

"He's got a point," Paul says, making me feel a little awkward that he is in agreement with Martin.

"You guys are both being ridiculous." I walk away before they can comment on my appearance any more. I walk out of the main room and go to my office, which just happens to be the room that Jake fucked me senseless in not so long ago. I unlock and open my office door, closing it behind me once I have walked in. I can still picture Jake and I, against the back wall, passion controlling our encounter. A shiver of delight goes through me at the thought. I smile and make my way over to my desk to check my phone. I unlock the screen and see that I have no new missed calls or texts. The smile quickly disappears from my face and turns into a scowl. I fire off a quick text to Jake.

Hey babe. I miss you like crazy. Tonight is going well, but it's not the same without you. I know that you have to work, but hurry up and come home! I love you.

Stace xxx.

I put my phone back on the desk and leave my office closing, and locking, the door behind me. I walk back down the corridor to the main room. I stand at the entrance to the main room, and scan my eyes around the place to make sure everything is still running smoothly. The dance floor is packed. The crowd go wild as the DJ starts to play Another Level, Freak Me. I smile and tap my foot in time to the beat. I watch as Lydia and Paul start to bump and grind together. They seem to be getting things back on track between them which is brilliant. My eyes find Martin next, and I break out in laughter as I see that he is, basically, humping a bar stool. His dance moves leave a lot to be desired. The staff are still busy at the bar. It will be interesting to see how much money we have taken tonight. I am about to go and give them a hand behind the bar, when I feel two hands grip my waist from behind. I freeze and my heartbeat starts to accelerate. I go to turn my head, but a hand comes up and grips me by my nape, meaning that I have to stay facing forward. I am gently pulled backwards so that my back comes into contact with a firm, hard chest. I keep my head facing forward as the hand that was holding my nape trails down the side of my neck, sweeping my hair to one side. Heated breath warms my skin and teeth start to nibble at my ear lobe. The hand returns to my waist and two arms lock around my midriff. I moan as light kisses are placed along my neck and back to my ear.

"Hey baby. Did you miss me?" Jake's voice purrs in my ear. I reach one hand up and place it behind his neck, turning my face to look at him. I smile as I drown in his caramel depths. *He's here! I can't believe that he's here!* Butterflies are going crazy in my stomach and I feel a little light headed. I pull his head down and I angle my head so that I can feel his lips against mine. Our lips connect and nothing else in the room exists. I open my mouth to him and let our tongues dance together. His hands loosen around my waist and I take that as my cue to turn my body to face him. Lips still connected, I turn in his arms and he clamps me to his body. I love the feel of him against me, and I love that I know that he is just as turned on as I am right now. His effect on me is powerful. I feel him smile against my lips and I pull my head back from him.

"I'll take that as a yes," he says, his eyes sparkling. I bury my face in his chest and enjoy just being held by him. I can't begin to describe my joy at him being here. He brings one hand to my chin and moves my head so that I am looking up at him.

"I missed you so much," I say to him.

"I can tell." He grins and I melt. The effect he has on me is still as strong as the day that I first met him.

"How come you didn't tell me that you were coming back tonight?" I ask.

"You know that I like to surprise you," he says with a wink.

"Oh Mr Waters, you are going to get so lucky when we get out of here."

"I was counting on it."

Chapter Two.

Stacey.

Jake and I are the last ones to leave The Den at just gone half three in the morning. It has been such a fantastic night, made all the better by Jake's surprise return. Everyone that I care about came to celebrate with me. I couldn't be happier right now. Eric is waiting by the limo, as usual, when we approach.

"Good evening Miss Stacey," Eric says, his normal greeting for me.

"More like good morning. I hope that he is paying you well Eric, dragging you out at this time," I say, playfully. This earns me a smack on my ass from Jake. I hear Eric laughing as I climb into the limo. Jake follows me and as soon as he is sat down, I straddle him. Luckily, the partition is up, meaning that Eric can't see my desperation for the man who is currently trapped between my legs.

"Someone's keen," Jake says with a cheeky smirk.

"And you're not?" I retaliate.

"Oh babe, it's been a week, I'm gonna blow your mind." My lips part at his suggestion and my whole body becomes aroused. Jake presses the button for the intercom and starts to speak to Eric. "Eric, would you mind driving around for a while?"

"No problem," Eric replies, his voice booming back through the speaker in the door.

"Why aren't we going straight home?" I question, frustration apparent in my tone.

"I can't wait until then. I need you, *now.*" *Oh my! Jake is certainly the sexiest predator that I have ever had the fortune to meet.*

"In here?" My eyebrows raise as I contemplate the thought of sex in the limo.

"That's right. Unless you don't want to?" Jake nibbles at my earlobe and I know that there is no way that I can resist him. His hands fondle my breasts, over my shirt, and I arch my back. Jake traces his tongue down my neck, and comes to a stop when he reaches my breast bone. He looks up at me with a wicked glint in his eyes and I melt. *Fuck, I really do love this man.* He smiles, which makes me quiver, and I can't wait any longer. I start to unbutton his shirt, needing to feel his bare chest. When his chest is exposed, I lean down and gently lick and suck his nipples in turn. I can hear a low rumble in his throat which turns me on even more. I move my hands to his trousers and unbuckle them as I slide my body down so that I am kneeling on the limo floor. I gaze up at him and see that he is trying to calm his breathing. I smile and snake my hand into his boxers, freeing his erection. I wrap my hand around the base and begin gentle strokes.

"Fuck yeah," Jake mutters. He closes his eyes and his head rolls back. I lower my head whilst he isn't looking and take him in my mouth. He groans in pleasure as I circle his tip with my tongue and then plunge his full length into my mouth, taking him all the way. "Ah, Jesus, that's good."

His words do things to my insides. I don't think that I will ever get my fill of this man. I increase my speed and his breathing quickens. I moan around his cock as I get ready to taste him. Just when I think that Jake is about to reach his climax, he pulls me off of him and gently shoves me onto the seat opposite. I whimper at the loss of him in my mouth. Before I can ask why he stopped me, his mouth crashes onto mine, rendering me speechless. Our embrace becomes frantic as we both crave the feel of each other after a week apart. Our tongues entwine, and our hands roam each other's bodies. He finally undoes my trousers and shimmies them down my legs, taking my knickers with them. I don't have any time to prepare myself as he plunges his length into me, hitting my core, and making me cry out from the feel of him inside me. My body is on fire as he pounds into me. With his powerful body on top of me, and his punishing rhythm hitting me just where I need it to, my climax gathers force. My hands fly into Jake's hair and my fingers tangle with his silky locks. I close my eyes as sensations tingle through me. Jake's heated breath is on my face and his lips find mine, kissing me as if our lives depend on it.

"Eyes baby. Let me see your eyes," Jake says, inches from my face. As hard as it is to open my eyes, I do, and I am penetrated by Jake's heated stare. His jaw is tense and I know that he is close to his release. My hands move up to his face, cupping his cheeks, his light stubble grazing against my palms. I tilt my head and place a soft kiss on his lips. The moment is so tender, despite our erratic love making. Jake groans as I pull my lips away.

"I love you," I whisper, emotion pulsing through me.

"Oh god," he says, holding my gaze as I feel his release pump inside of me. This triggers my own climax, and together, we ride out the height of our pleasure. Jake buries his face in my neck as we both lie there, panting, trying to catch our breath. *That was awesome.* As I lie there, in my post orgasmic state, I run my fingernails up and down Jake's back, enjoying the feel of goose-bumps rising on his skin.

"I can't believe we just did that," I say, suddenly embarrassed at my actions. Jake pulls his head up and places a kiss on the end of my nose.

"Well believe it babe. I'm going away more often if I get a welcome home like that every time." I swat Jake's arm with my hand and I hear a rumble of laughter deep in his throat.

"It's not funny Jake. What if Eric heard us?"

"So what if he did?" Jake seems completely unfazed.

"I'll never be able to look him in the eye again. I blame you for this."

"You blame me?" Jake raises his eyebrows in question.

"Yes. It's your fault for being so bloody handsome," I say, knowing that he will love that answer. He gives me the most gorgeous smile, and if we hadn't already had sex, then that smile would most definitely make me do naughty things to him despite my embarrassment at the possibility of us being heard. I feel his cock twitch within me and my eyes widen in surprise. *He can't possibly be ready to go again?*

"Maybe we should get back home now," Jake says, pulling out of me. He sits back on the opposite seat to me as I sit myself up and start to make myself look presentable.

"I think that is a good idea," I reply. Jake speaks to Eric through the intercom and asks him to take us back to the house. Jake switches the intercom off and then looks at me, heat blazing in his eyes.

"When we get home, I'm going to take my time with you. I want to taste every inch of you." I gasp and my sex, which hasn't calmed down from round one yet, tingles in anticipation. Jake gestures for me to sit on his lap, and I happily comply. I place my arms around his neck and Jake cups my face in his hands. "I'm going to make love to you, worship you, and make you scream." I bite my lip to stop myself from moaning out loud. Jake's eyes are hungry, and I am sure that the same feeling is reflected in mine. He runs his tongue across my bottom lip and I shiver with delight, imagining what he is going to do to me when we get home.

"I can't wait," I whisper.

Chapter Three.

Stacey.

I am up, showered and dressed before Jake is awake. I have only had a few hours' sleep, and as much as I want to spend longer in bed with Jake, I have to go to The Den. My limbs ache, but in a good way. Jake wasn't exaggerating when he said he was going to worship me and make me scream last night. I lost count of how many times he brought me to orgasm. We made love in the hall way, in the shower, and in our bed. Jake took his time with me, almost torturing me with desire. Our love making last night was deeper and more meaningful than it has been before. I'm not quite sure how, it just was. Jake and I have always had an amazing sex life, but last night surpassed every other time. I smile as I write a note for Jake, telling him that I have had to leave and that I didn't want to disturb him. I leave the note on the front of the coffee machine, as that will be the first place Jake goes when he wakes up. I make myself a coffee, put it in my travel mug, pick up my handbag and keys, and leave our house. I get into my car with a bounce in my step. I put my seatbelt on, start the car, and turn the music on. The smooth sounds of Usher fills the sound system. I wind down my window as it is already hot, even though it is only ten o clock. I put my sunglasses on and I pull off of the drive way. I sing along to 'Caught Up' as I drive along. I feel great. All of the sexual release last night has done wonders for my mood.

The drive doesn't take long, and I am soon pulling into the car park for The Den. Now that I am the manager, I have my own designated parking space. There are definitely some perks to running this place. I get out of my car, grab my handbag and travel mug, and head for the back door of the building. I enter, disable the alarm, and lock the door behind me. I go to my office and find the relevant key to unlock it. I keep the office locked at all times when I am not here. I don't want any of the staff, or god forbid customers, to be able to walk in and do whatever they like. I unlock the door and enter, going straight to my desk and putting my handbag down. I then go to the main room to check that the place is clean and tidy for opening time later. The cleaners come in early every morning, escorted by a security guard. The security guard has keys, but the cleaners don't. I didn't want to start dishing keys out to just anybody. It may seem a little bit silly, and I know that Caitlin is no longer around, but you can never be too careful about who you trust. The security guard is a guy that used to work for Jake at Waters Industries, and if Jake trusts him, then that is good enough for me. I look around the main room and admire the way the place looks. I really did work hard to bring this place up to scratch. The bar stools are almost gleaming and the black glass table tops shine. Satisfied with the upkeep, I take a sip of my coffee and return to my office. I leave the office door open and go to my desk. I sit down, loving how comfortable my chair is, and I fire up my laptop. I take a look at the rota for the coming week and feel deflated as I look at it. I am working every evening until next Monday, something that I haven't yet told Jake. I hope that he understands, being a business man, that I need to be here for the time being. I want this place to be successful. I feel like I need to prove to myself that I can do this. I have Lydia and Susie working tonight, along with two new temps called Stephanie and Darren. I am going to be here to supervise and help train the temps to see if they are suitable for bar work. Stephanie has no experience, but she seemed likeable, so I thought that I would give her a chance. She is only twenty-two, and although a little shy, she assured me that she could hold her own. Only time will tell I guess. Darren was a completely different kettle of fish. He's thirty-two, and he has done bar work since leaving college. I decided to give him a shot due to his experience, and the fact that he's a little easy on the eye. Not my type, but I think that the ladies will like him. It may seem a bit shallow of me but I need to think about what is best for business. Stephanie and Darren are the only temps that I have hired so far and I really need to pencil in some time to hire a couple more staff members. I just haven't had time to interview anyone else, what with the re-modelling of the place. I get my diary out of my desk draw and look to see when I am free to conduct interviews. I literally have no time this week, so I resign myself to the fact that I am going to have to keep using agency staff to fill the void for the time being. I make a note in my diary to advertise for some more temps as soon as possible. I am about to take a look at the profit for last night, when my phone starts ringing. I take it out of my handbag and answer, without checking who it is calling me.

"Hello, Stacey Paris," I say, in an official tone just in case it is work related.

"Babes, why the fuck are you being formal?" Lydia's voice says. Never one to sugar coat her words.

"Oh, hey Lyd. Sorry, I answered without checking who was calling. What's up?" I ask her.

"I need to talk to you. It's urgent." A feeling of dread creeps up my spine at her words. Please don't say that she has had a setback. She has been doing so well since her episode with drugs that I find myself hoping that she hasn't taken anything.

"Okay. Where are you now?"

"Stacey Marie Paris, you took far too long to answer me. I know what you are thinking, and no, I haven't taken anything." She knows me far too well.

"I wasn't……."

"Don't try and bullshit me lady, I have known you far too long," Lydia says, cutting me off before I can try and defend myself. I almost feel like a naughty school girl who has just been caught smoking behind the sports block.

"Sorry. I shouldn't have thought that you would do that." There is no point in trying to excuse what I was thinking. It would only piss Lydia off if I was to lie to her.

"It's okay. I would have thought the same if it had been the other way around. Anyway, where are you?" she says, changing the subject.

"I'm at The Den, but I can leave and be with you in ten minutes?"

"No, no. I'll come to you. Nick's at the flat, and I need to talk to you without anyone else around. I have my keys on me and I will be as quick as I can."

"Okay Lyd. See you soon."

"Bye babes," she says and hangs up the phone. I wonder what could be so urgent that she needs to see me right now. If it's not the drugs thing, then I can only guess that it is Paul related. God, I hope that things haven't gone wrong between them. They have been getting on so well recently. They make a cute couple and he actually treats her with respect. I turn my attention back to the computer screen and bring up the profit count for last night. The amount made is far more than I had predicted. I feel a sense of achievement, but I know that I have to work hard to keep the profit up. I understand that, being opening night last night, the profit would probably be more than it would be on a normal night, but I still need to aim high. My phone starts to ring, interrupting me again. This time I look at the screen and see that Jake is calling me. I feel a tingle go through me as I answer the call.

"Good morning Mr Waters," I purr into the phone.

"Don't you good morning me Miss Paris." Oh dear, he doesn't sound very happy.

"What's wrong with you?" I ask, wondering what could have possibly put him in a bad mood.

"Why the bloody hell didn't you wake me up this morning?"

"Because you were sleeping, duh." I can't help but sound sarcastic.

"Not in the mood Stace."

"Oh cheer up stroppy. What's bit you in the ass?"

"Well, let's see, I was hoping to be woken up by my sexy, beautiful girlfriend this morning but instead, I get left a crappy note. I envisioned us spending the day together, preferably naked, but obviously not." He really is in a sulk. At the mention of us naked in bed together, my sex stirs. I squeeze my legs together and try to shut down the ache, deep within me.

"Listen here Waters, your girlfriend is very busy running one of *your* businesses. *If* you had told me that you were coming back last night, then I could have got today covered, but you didn't. I'd say that's bad planning on your part baby." I know that I am fuelling his annoyance, but I love to tease him. I can hear him breathing down the phone and it makes my body shiver.

"You just wait until I get my hands on you Miss Paris."

"I will look forward to it," I whisper into the phone before I cut the call. I smirk at the fact that he is going to be wound up all day now. Excellent. He will be like an animal by the time I get home tonight. My sex quivers with excitement at what will await me. I shake my head and pull myself from my fantasy and return my attention to my computer screen. I print out some of the paperwork for Stephanie and Darren to look through before they start their shift tonight. Sipping my coffee, I sit back and my eyes go to the picture of Jake and I on my desk. He is standing behind me, with his arms wrapped around me. Our heads are angled so that we are staring into each other's eyes, and we both look so happy. I smile and think about how lucky I am, when I hear the back door open and slam shut. I jolt out of my thoughts and sit up straight. My heart starts to pound a little. I listen carefully and that's when I hear Lydia curse before she strides into my office. I flop back in my chair with relief. I don't know who I was expecting to see other than her. The only people with keys are myself, Jake, Lydia and one of the security guards. I need to stop being so jittery. *Caitlin is gone, behind bars. She isn't coming back here for you.* I take in Lydia's frazzled state as she flops down on the sofa opposite me. She is breathing heavy and looks a little wind swept.

"Jeez, did you sprint here or something?" I ask her.

"Pretty much," she says as she tries to catch her breath.

"Really?" Lydia never runs, so I know that whatever she needs to tell me must be serious. She nods at me and I see that her eyes are puffy. She has been crying. She also looks a little pale. "Lyd, what's wrong?" She looks at me, and her eyes mist with tears. *Oh shit.* I put my coffee down and walk over to her. I take a seat by her on the sofa and put my arm around her shoulders. "Oh god, what is it Lyd?" Tears start to fall down her cheeks and she looks at me like she is in pain. I wait, for what feels like an eternity for her to speak, but when she does, her words shock the hell out of me.

“I’m pregnant.”

Chapter Four.

Stacey.

After getting over my initial shock at Lydia's news, I manage to find my voice.

"Are you sure?" I ask her.

"I did six separate tests Stace. They can't all be wrong." *Well, no-one can accuse her of not being thorough!*

"No, I guess not. Have you made a doctor's appointment yet?" It seems like the next logical question to ask.

"Yeah. I go this afternoon at three."

"I'm coming with you." She smiles and I know that she is grateful for my support.

"What the hell am I going to do Stace? I'm just getting my life back on track, and now this." She looks to me for an answer, but I don't have one. I just stare at her blankly. "Oh god," she says and hangs her head in her hands.

"What made you think that you were pregnant in the first place?"

"I've been feeling sick the last few mornings, and this morning I threw up. I only had a couple of glasses of champagne last night, so I couldn't understand why I felt so bad, and then it hit me. With my head down the toilet, it hit me. My period is also a few days late, but I just put that down to stress from recent events." She takes a deep, shaky breath, and looks at me. "I rushed out this morning and bought some pregnancy tests, and, hey presto, the little window of truth confirmed it."

"Shit." My response isn't great, but I don't know what else to say.

"I know. Talk about terrible fucking timing." Lydia lets out a sigh.

"Oh my god, is Paul the dad?" I ask her. She doesn't answer me, but the look on her face tells me all that I need to know. "You don't know, do you?" She shakes her head and fresh tears fall down her cheeks. "Oh Lyd," I say as I pull her into a hug. My mobile phone starts to ring, but I ignore it. Whoever it is can wait. My phone stops ringing, and then my office phone starts to ring.

"Don't you want to get that?" Lydia asks me.

"No." I move off of the sofa and go to my private toilet to get Lydia some tissues. I return to her and hand her a bunch of them.

"Thanks," she says as she wipes at her eyes.

"Do you want a drink?" I ask her.

"Sure." I leave my office and go to the main room, making my way behind the bar. I grab two bottles of water from the fridge and then I place them on the side. I rest my hands against the bar and try to process my thoughts. Poor Lydia. She has just got herself to a good place in her life, and now she has this bombshell to deal with. I hope, for her sake, that Paul is the father. I dread to think what will happen if it is that Callum guy, or even worse, Donnie. The thought makes me shudder and I quickly push it away, reasoning that Donnie has been gone for a while now so it couldn't be his baby. My thoughts are interrupted, and I jump in shock, as the front door to The Den bursts open. I squeal in surprise and stand there looking dumbfounded as Jake comes marching in. He sweeps his eyes across the room, before they land on me behind the bar.

"Why the fuck aren't you answering the phone?" his face is like thunder. *His day clearly isn't getting any better yet.*

"Because, it's in my office and I am out here," I reply, annoyed that he has come bursting in here and scared me half to death.

"For Christ sake woman, I was worried that something had happened to you." Jake reaches the bar and walks behind. He comes towards me and pulls me to him, enveloping me in his arms. I relax against his body, loving the feel of him. In Jake's arms, I always feel safe. I breath in his scent and then lean my head back to look at him.

"Sorry. I didn't mean to worry you." I move back so that I am resting against the bar. Jake's hands move to either side of me, resting on the bar, effectively encasing me. "Why didn't you just check the cameras? You have access to them. Would that not have been easier than storming in here like a raging bull?" Jake had high tech cameras installed during the re-modelling, allowing him to monitor them from his computer.

"I wasn't in the office or at home, so I have no access to either computers to check the damn cameras."

"Oh." I'm flattered that he was worried about me, but his reaction is a little dramatic. His stare is penetrating me as I look up at him from under my lashes. *God, I could get lost in those eyes all day long.* My body reacts to him, without me even telling it to. My nipples harden and I feel a warmth spread through me. I push off of the bar and place a light kiss on his lips. He moves closer and leans into me, his crotch pressing against my stomach. I sigh at the feel of him and it takes all of my willpower not to rip his clothes off. I clench my jaw and see that Jake is doing the same thing, his eyes blazing with desire. I clear my throat and find my voice again, needing to diffuse this sexually charged moment, seeing as Lydia is in my office and could walk out at any minute.

"So, now that you have checked on me, don't you have a company to run?"

"Mmmmm." He steps back slightly, and grabs one of the water bottles off of the bar, opening it and taking a few gulps. His eyes are drawn back to the second bottle and he stops drinking. "Is someone here with you?" he asks.

"Yeah. It's my lover." I can't resist the urge to tease him. His face quickly turns into a scowl and I stifle a giggle that has worked its way up my throat.

"Not funny Stace."

"What?" I feign innocence.

"You know what," he replies, his voice sounding dangerous, causing my skin to tingle.

"Okay, okay." I decide to back down now. I think I may have wound him up enough already today. "Lydia is in my office."

"Oh right. Is everything okay?"

"Yeah. We're just going over the rota for the coming week." I feel awful not telling him about Lydia being pregnant, but I don't know if she wants others to know about it yet.

"Well in that case, I will leave you guys to it. How about I cook for us tonight and we can have a quiet evening?" His question is loaded with expectation, and I know that I am about to piss him off with my answer.

"I would love to, but……"

"Oh no, please don't tell me that you're working?" he says, cutting me off.

"Unfortunately, I am." He sighs in frustration and runs his hand through his hair. "I'm sorry, but I need to help train the new temps tonight."

"Fuck sake." I step forwards and press my body up against him whilst linking my arms around his neck. I tilt my head so that my lips are angled to touch his. I lightly brush my lips across his and then I let my tongue dart out, licking his bottom lip.

"I will make it up to you when I get home." I make my tone as enticing as possible and that is all it takes for Jake to wrap his arms around me and lift me up his body. I instinctively wrap my legs around his waist and crash my lips down on his. I savour the taste of him, knowing that I won't see him until late tonight. When we finally come up for air, I run my hands through his locks.

"I promise that it will be worth the wait," I whisper, enjoying the feel of his hands cupping my ass.

"Oh I have no doubt about that. I just don't like that I have to wait so long." I laugh at him as he pouts at me.

"I know." He releases me and my legs slide down his body until I am standing on my feet again.

"The things you do to me woman." I smile and he starts to walk out from behind the bar. "I love you," he says as he walks towards the front doors.

"I love you too." He turns around, smiles and then opens the front door, disappearing out of it. I sigh and grab the bottles of water. That man can turn me to putty in his hands, most of the time. I tingle with delight as I walk back to my office. I know that tonight will be a night worth waiting for.

Chapter Five.

Stacey.

The doctor's waiting room clock reads 14:56. It's nearly time for Lydia's appointment. I know that she is nervous as her leg is twitching up and down like crazy.

"Calm down Lyd, everything is going to be okay," I try to reassure her. She doesn't acknowledge me, but she does stop the leg twitching. Lydia's name is called out a few seconds later and she stands up.

"Will you come in with me?" she asks, looking pale.

"Of course." As if she even had to ask me. I follow her to the correct room and Lydia knocks on the door.

"Come in," a male voice says on the other side. Lydia takes a deep breath and pushes the door open, me following behind her. I close the door when I have entered the room, and I follow Lydia to the seats in front of the doctor's desk. I sit in the left-hand seat and my eyes lock with the doctor's. *Wow! He's handsome.* He smiles warmly at me, which I return. His looks are striking. He has short, black, cropped hair, and a strong jaw line. There is no stubble on his chin, giving him the appearance of baby soft, smooth skin. His skin is lightly tanned, but it is his eyes that give him his stunning quality. They are brown, but they appear to have gold flecks in them. I feel a little bit guilty assessing another man, but no one can hold up against Jake.

"Good afternoon ladies," the doctor says. "I'm Doctor Bradley. Which one of you is Lydia?"

"I am," Lydia answers in a small, quiet voice. "This is my friend Stacey." Lydia points at me, as if it wasn't already obvious.

"Hi," I say, not wanting to appear ignorant.

"Nice to meet you Stacey," Doctor Bradley replies. He turns his attention back to Lydia. "So, Lydia, what can I do for you today?"

"Well, I'm, um....." she stops and closes her eyes, taking a deep breath. "I'm pregnant," she says, only opening her eyes after she has spoken those words.

"Okay. I'm guessing that, by the look on your face, that this isn't a planned pregnancy?" he asks.

"No," Lydia replies.

"Right. Well Lydia, I need you to do a urine sample for me. It's so that I can confirm your pregnancy for our records." Doctor Bradley pulls open one of the draws on his desk, and produces a urine sample container. He holds it out to Lydia and she stares at him, looking shocked.

"You want me to do it now?" she asks.

"If you feel that you are able to, then yes, please." I hear Lydia gulp as she reaches for the pot. She looks at me nervously, and I smile and nod my head trying to encourage her. She rises from her chair, and I watch her leave the room, the door clicking shut behind her. I turn back to face the doctor and he is looking at me. I sit there feeling slightly awkward and avert my gaze. I don't really know what to say, so I pull my phone out of my bag and I pretend to type out a text message for something to do. Doctor Bradley doesn't speak, but I can feel his gaze on me. If that was Jake sat there, looking at me, I would be on cloud nine, but, although this doctor is handsome, it is just making me feel uncomfortable. After what feels like forever, Lydia returns, and I put my phone away, feeling grateful that she has come back into the room. She hands the sample pot to the doctor.

"Thank you Lydia," he says, taking the pot off of her. She sits back down in her seat and looks at me. I put my hand on hers and give it a squeeze as Doctor Bradley walks over to a sideboard and pulls out a little strip of paper. I watch as he pops on a pair of latex gloves, opens the pot, and dips the strip of paper into the urine for a few seconds. He then pulls the paper out, looks at his watch and waits. I watch the clock on the wall and three minutes later, Doctor Bradley throws the strip of paper away and disposes of the pot and its contents. He pulls the gloves off, throwing those away too, and washes his hands before coming to sit back down.

"Well, you were right Lydia. Congratulations, you are indeed pregnant." Lydia doesn't move a muscle, but her eyes start to mist over. The doctor notices and starts to speak again. "Lydia, if this isn't something that you want, then you do have other options." He speaks in a soft and gentle voice, obviously realising the sensitivity of the situation. I hold my breath at his words. The doctor clearly hasn't looked back at Lydia's medical history. If he had, then he would see that this is a topic that would affect Lydia, badly. Lydia had an abortion when she was sixteen, and she has told me that it was the hardest decision that she has ever had to make. I can't begin to imagine what she must have gone through. Lydia lets a few tears fall down her cheeks and the doctor starts to pull some pamphlets out of another draw at his desk. He places them on the top of the desk and I quickly whip them away, shoving them into my hand bag. Doctor Bradley furrows his brows at me, obviously wondering why I have been the one to snatch the pamphlets away.

"Uh, thanks," I say, not knowing how else to respond. I smile awkwardly and I know that he is assessing my behaviour. I couldn't really give a shit what he thinks, I just know that I need to get Lydia out of here as soon as possible. Doctor Bradley clears his throat and then starts to ask Lydia a series of questions. Lydia answers every question, and I know that she is as desperate to leave here as I am.

"I will need to book you an appointment with the midwife. Is there any particular time that is good for you Lydia?" he asks whilst looking at his computer screen. She looks to me and I answer for her.

"Anytime is fine," I reply and the doctor looks up at me, once again looking confused. "I'm her boss," I say with a shrug of my shoulders as a way of an explanation. He nods at me and looks back at the computer. He writes down an appointment time on a card and hands it to Lydia.

“Thanks,” she says as she stands up. I follow suit, and so does Doctor Bradley. He holds his hand out to Lydia and she shakes it quickly before turning and heading for the door. I am about to follow her, when Doctor Bradley thrusts his hand in my direction. I hesitate for a moment before taking his hand. He’s looking at me, and I feel a bit silly for feeling awkward so I try to shake off my weird feeling. His grip is firm as he shakes my hand and his thumb brushes my wrist. I pull my hand away as quick as I can and mutter a good bye as I go to leave the room. Lydia has already gone, and as I go to close the door, Doctor Bradley speaks.

“See you soon Stacey,” he says. I don’t know why he has said it. Shouldn’t he have said that to Lydia? She is his patient after all. I don’t know how to respond so I give a nod of my head and close the door, breathing a sigh of relief as I get outside and inhale the fresh air. *Why the hell did I just feel so awkward in there?* I look for Lydia and see that she is stood by my car, waiting for me to join her. I unlock the doors and we both, silently, get in. I look across to Lydia, and she just looks deflated.

“Hey,” I say softly. “How are you feeling?”

“Like crap.” She runs her fingers through her wild hair, and sighs. “Thank you for cutting the abortion talk short. I know that I was only young when I first got pregnant, and I know that it was the right thing to do, but it is still painful to think about it.”

“I know.” I start the car and put my seatbelt on. “Listen, I’m going to cover our shifts at the bar tonight……”

"No Stace, you don't have to do that," Lydia says, cutting me off.

"Yes I do. You are coming to my house and staying the night. No arguments." I start to drive out of the car park and turn in the direction of my place.

"Stace, you have the temps coming in tonight. You have to be there."

"No I don't. Susie can show them what to do." I sound more confident than I feel. I really should be there, but Lydia needs me more right now.

"But, won't Jake mind?"

"Of course he won't." *Yes, he will.* Lydia goes silent for a few moments, and I think that she is going to try and talk me out of covering our shifts, but she surprises me.

"Thanks Stace. I couldn't face going back to the flat right now." I look over at her and see some relief across her face. I smile at her and turn my attention back to the road. I'm pretty sure that Jake is going to be really pissed off, but I can't worry about that. "Stace?" Lydia says, interrupting my thoughts.

"Hmm?"

"Please don't tell Jake that I'm pregnant. I don't want anyone else to know yet." I hesitate to answer her. I don't want to have to lie to Jake. Lydia must sense my discomfort. "Please Stace. I need to work it out in my head first. I also don't want to run the risk of Paul finding out before I have had the chance to speak to him." I can hear the desperation in her voice and my heart goes out to her.

"Okay," I say. "I won't tell Jake." I look across to her and she smiles.

"Thank you." I turn my attention back to the road. *How the hell am I going to keep this from Jake? I'm going to have to pull off some major acting skills so that he doesn't see that I am hiding something from him.*

Chapter Six.

Stacey.

Lydia and I are sitting at the kitchen island, drinking hot chocolate. I have just got off of the phone to Susie who is more than happy to show the temps the ropes tonight. I have also contacted some agency staff to come in tonight to cover Lydia and myself. The last call I need to make is to Jake. I scroll through the names on my phone until I find him, and I am about to press the button to call him, when I hear the front door open. I hear Jake talking, followed by another male voice. I look at Lydia and she has paled considerably.

"Oh shit," she says as realisation dawns on me that the other male voice is Paul. "Paul can't see me Stace. I can't speak to him right now." The desperation in her voice makes me jump into action.

"It's okay, I'll get rid of him." I hop off of the stool and practically sprint to the kitchen door. I need a really good reason for not wanting Paul here. *Think Stacey, think!* Jake and Paul have their backs to me, as I enter the hall way. I close the kitchen door behind me and they both turn around.

"Hi guys," I say, a little too high pitched.

"Hi Stace," Paul says. I give a little wave as I continue to rack my brains for a good excuse.

"Stace? I thought you were working tonight?" Jake asks.

"Oh, um, I was, but, uh......" *Oh Christ, he's going to know that something is wrong if I don't form a sentence quick.* It is at that moment that the excuse I need enters my head. And that excuse consists of making Jake think that I came home to spend some *alone* time with him.

"Is everything okay?" Jake asks, looking a little perplexed.

"Oh yeah. Everything's fine. I just......I covered my shift so that we could, you know, spend some time together." Jake raises one eyebrow at me and puts his hands in the pockets of his trousers.

"Is that right?" he says, his mouth twitching as he clearly tries to hold back a smile.

"Um, yes. I just thought that we could have made the most of tonight as I'm working every other night this week, but, it doesn't matter. I guess I should have called you earlier, but, um, sorting out cover for my shift took longer than I thought." I try to sound as convincing as possible. Paul starts to fidget on the spot and I feel a little bit guilty about lying to both of them. "So, what do you guys have planned then?" Hopefully it isn't too important and Jake will ask Paul to leave.

"Not much. Just thought that we would have a few beers and watch some sports," Jake replies.

"Oh," I answer. "Okay." *Just sports. Nothing too dramatic.* "Well, I will just go and have a long soak in the bath and let you guys enjoy your evening." At the mention of having a bath, Jake's eyes light up and I sense that I might be getting somewhere. I make my way to the stairs, giving Jake a quick kiss on the lips as I pass. I make it to the top of the first flight of stairs, when I hear mumbled voices coming from below. I can't make out what they are saying, but I pray that my feeble plan has worked. If it hasn't and they both walk into the kitchen and see Lydia sat there, they are going to know that something is going on. I continue to make my way to the second floor and head for mine and Jake's bedroom. I make my way to the bed, and am about to sit down and wait to see what happens, when I feel two hands grab me from behind, pulling me backwards. I connect with Jake's hard chest as he wraps his arms around me, nuzzling his face in my neck. I giggle as his stubble tickles and I squirm in his arms. He loosens his grip so that I can turn to face him before pining me on the bed, arms above my head. His eyes sparkle with mischief.

"So, you said something about a long soak in the bath?"

"I did, but shouldn't you be entertaining your guest?" I say as Jake rubs his nose against mine.

"Paul kindly left." I feel a pang of guilt. Jake lowers his lips to mine and kisses me, tenderly. I moan against his mouth, enjoying the sensation of his lips on mine. He lets go of my hands and I bring them to his chest. I push against his chest slightly, causing him to pull his head away from me.

"Jake, I need to tell you something," I say, feeling nervous.

"Okay." He looks at me with those intoxicating eyes of his and I pray that he isn't going to be too pissed off with me.

"Um, I may have told a little white lie, just now, downstairs."

"What do you mean?" Jake asks. He moves off of me and sits on the edge of the bed. I sit up so that I am beside him.

"Well, I wasn't completely honest about the real reason that I covered my shift tonight." Jake doesn't say anything, clearly waiting for me to expand on my answer. *Oh boy, here goes.* "I couldn't tell you the real reason before because Paul was there." He frowns at me, clearly wondering why Paul being here would be a problem. "Lydia is currently sat in our kitchen and she didn't want to see Paul, but obviously, I couldn't tell you guys that just now. I was about to call you as you walked in the front door. She's staying here tonight." I am well aware that I am rambling right now.

"Hold on a sec. Why doesn't she want to see Paul? I thought that those two were doing good now?"

"They are, she just, um……" I rack my brains for why the hell she wouldn't want to see him. I don't want to have to lie to Jake about why, but I've promised Lydia that I will keep her pregnancy a secret. I decide to be as honest as I can, considering I lied to him a few minutes ago. "I can't tell you."

"Why the hell not?"

"I just can't. I'm sorry, but, I promised Lydia."

"But, it's me Stace. You can tell me anything." Oh god, does he have to make me feel guiltier than I already do?

"Yes I know that I can. It's not that I don't trust you, I just can't break my promise to Lydia."

"For fuck sake," Jake mutters as he stands up and runs his fingers through his hair. He walks into the ensuite and takes his jacket off, throwing it into the washing basket. *Oh yeah, he's pissed.* I watch him as he turns the shower on and starts to undress himself. He doesn't look at me, and then he disappears out of my view as he enters the shower. *Bugger. I knew he would be annoyed but I thought that he would understand why I had to lie and why I can't tell him anything.* I run down the stairs to the kitchen to check on Lydia. I open the kitchen door and see that she is still sat at the kitchen island. She turns around at the sound of someone entering and looks relieved that it is me.

"Oh thank god it's you," she says.

"Don't worry. Paul's gone." She smiles at me and I try to return it, but my mind is on Jake right now. "Do you mind just chilling in the lounge for a bit whilst I speak to Jake?"

"Sure babes. Is Jake okay?" She gets off of the stool and walks over to me.

"He will be."

"Oh no, I don't want to cause problems for you. I'll just go back to the flat Stace......."

"No you won't," I say, cutting her off. "Jake will be fine." I walk to the lounge, Lydia following me. I pick up the television remote and hand it to her. "You make yourself at home and I won't be long."

"But......"

"No buts Lydia. Now, I'm just going to go and soothe a man's ego and then I will cook us some food and, after, we can watch a film." I wink at her as I leave to the sound of her chuckling. I race back up the stairs and see that Jake is still in the shower. *Good.* I close our bedroom door and strip my clothes off. I enter the ensuite and see that Jake has his back to me. I quietly climb into the shower, standing behind him, and admire his naked form. *God, he really does have an ass to die for.* I, carefully, make my way over to him. As I reach him, I place my hands on his shoulders and start to trace light kisses across his back. Jake stops washing himself and I feel his body respond to me. I kiss my way down to his ass, my hands going around to the front of his thighs. I move my body around his legs so that I am kneeling in front of him, the water pounding on top of me. I close my eyes to shield them from the water, and I take his length in my mouth. I place my hands on his ass and caress his gloriously smooth skin. His hands run through my, now sodden, hair and I lick and suck him, making him groan in pleasure. I hear his breathing quicken and I increase the pressure, knowing that he is close to climax.

"Stace," he says on a whisper as he explodes into my mouth. I suck him gently, swallowing all of his juices. When I have wrung him dry, I release his length and kiss my way up his torso, running my hands up the sides of his body. I kiss his neck and along his jaw line, finding my way to his lips. He pulls me close to his body and our tongues entwine. Our kiss is gentle and loving. I gently bite his bottom lip before pulling away and wiping the water from my eyes so that I can look at him.

"I love you," I whisper, overcome with the intensity of his eyes on mine.

"I love you too." I rest my head against his chest.

"I'm sorry that I lied, and I'm sorry that I can't tell you what's going on with Lydia."

"Sssshh." He places a hand under my chin and moves my head so that I am looking at him. "Don't apologise, it's fine. I didn't mean to act like a prick earlier. I just miss having you to myself."

"I miss that too." I smile at him and I see that any annoyance that he may have had, about the situation, has dissipated. He lowers his head to mine and kisses me, taking my breath away. I feel his cock harden against my stomach and I break away from his lips, raising my eyebrows in question. "Really?" He just smiles at me, confirming all I needed to know and I lose myself in his embrace. Right now, in this moment, this is the only place that I want to be.

Chapter Seven.

Stacey.

Jake, Lydia and I are all sat at the dining table, ready to eat the lasagne that I have just finished cooking. Jake has been more relaxed since our escapade in the shower. He has been laughing and joking with Lydia and I, and I think that Lydia's mood has lifted somewhat.

"This looks great Stace," Lydia says as she licks her lips at the sight of the food on the table.

"It's just lasagne and garlic bread Lyd," I reply. "Go ahead and help yourself." Lydia wastes no time in filling her whole plate with lasagne, as well as taking a couple of slices of garlic bread. I watch in amazement as she starts to shovel the food into her mouth. It's like she hasn't eaten for days. Jake was putting food on his plate, but his hand has frozen in mid-air at the sight of Lydia. I nudge him, under the table, with my foot. He looks to me and I indicate for him to stop staring. Luckily, Lydia hasn't noticed anything. She seems far too interested in the food to take any notice of us. Jake finishes spooning lasagne onto his plate, handing the serving spoon to me. I take a spoonful and then a slice of garlic bread. Lydia has already demolished half of her plateful before I have even taken my first bite. She's going to give away her secret if she keeps eating like that.

"So, what film do you fancy watching later Lyd?" I ask her, trying to take the attention away from her hoovering up her food.

"I don't mind," she replies, taking another slice of garlic bread. *Huh. Well, that cut that conversation short.* I look to Jake and his eyes have returned to watching Lydia. I roll my own eyes and start to eat my own food. We all remain silent whilst we eat which makes me feel a little awkward. I don't like how uncomfortable the atmosphere is right now. I also don't understand it. I just want to finish this meal and get the hell away from the table.

"Fair play Stace," Lydia says as she eats her last mouthful, "that was tasty. Does anyone mind if I have some more?" she looks to both of us and I hear Jake scoff in surprise. I nudge him again, with my foot, and he scowls at me. I smile sweetly, not wanting Lydia to feel embarrassed.

"No, you go ahead Lyd," I answer. Lydia dishes out the remaining lasagne and, literally, inhales it. I put my fork down, having lost my appetite, and take a gulp of my wine. I patiently wait for Jake and Lydia to finish, and then I busy myself by clearing the table.

"That's better. I was starving," Lydia declares.

"Glad you enjoyed it," Jake manages to respond, and I can hear him stifling his laughter. He glugs back his beer and goes to the fridge to get another one.

“Why don’t you go through to the lounge Lyd? I’m just going to finish cleaning up in here and then I’ll come and join you.”

“If you insist.” Lydia gets up and leaves the room, rubbing her belly as she does. Jake looks at me and mouths the words, ‘oh my god.’ I roll my eyes at him and I start to load the plates into the dishwasher. Jake waits patiently for me to finish and then pulls me through the patio doors and out into the garden.

“What the hell was that about?” he asks me, surprise and amusement evident in his tone.

“What was what about?” I feign ignorance.

“You know what. She just inhaled her food in there, barely stopping for breath.” He looks astonished, and it takes all of my skills to keep my face neutral.

“Don’t be silly. She was just hungry.” I really hope that he doesn’t say too much more on the subject. I hate not being able to tell him.

“Hungry? Jesus, I thought that she was going to eat the tablecloth at one point.” I bite my lip to stop myself from laughing.

“Jake, don’t be so mean,” I say, the chuckle escaping into the back of my throat.

“I’m not, but, come on babe, that was something else.” He bursts out laughing and I crumble. I’m not making fun of Lydia, I’m just laughing at the whole situation. The look on Jake’s face throughout that meal was a picture. I hold my stomach as the laughter starts to hurt.

"Stop it," I say as I try to catch my breath. "It's not funny."

"Oh, it is."

"Seriously." I wipe my eyes and the laughter starts to subside. One day, when Lydia has made her secret public knowledge, she will laugh about this with us. I know she will.

"Anyway, I'm going to my office to send some emails. If you two are watching a chick flick, then I would rather opt out."

"Okay. As long as you don't mind."

"Of course I mind," Jake says as he steps closer to me, invading my personal space. An invasion that I, most certainly, welcome. His arms go around my waist and I place my hands on his shoulders. "I wanted you all to myself, but seeing as we have company, I will just have to leave you with this….." His lips crash down on mine as his voice fades off. I mould myself against him, my nipples harden, my sex stirs, my senses come alive. One of his hands travels around my waist and heads south, skimming the hem of my skirt and trailing its way up the inside of my thigh. His fingers graze over my sex, rubbing, teasing. Sparks fly through my body. His gentle touch makes me want to rip his clothes off here and now. As I am losing my mind from his actions, Jake abruptly pulls away from me and steps back. I stand there, gasping, a little uncertain of how I was in his arms one minute and the next he is backing away from me. He smirks, doesn't say a word, and just walks back into the house. *What the hell? Why would he do that? Why would he just……* The realisation hits me like a lightning bolt. *Ah, I get it. Mr Waters wants to play games.* He is clearly showing me a taste of what I will be missing seeing as we won't be on our own tonight. Getting over my initial shock at his abrupt departure, I start to smile. *If Mr Waters wants to play, that's fine by me. Bring it on.*

I walk back into the house and go through to the lounge. Lydia is sprawled out on the sofa, watching The Notebook which is one of my favourite films. I flop down beside her, suddenly feeling tired from the day's events.

"I take it that Jake is okay with me staying here?" Lydia asks me.

"Of course he is. I told you earlier that he would be fine."

"I feel guilty that I am making you keep my pregnancy a secret from him."

"Don't worry," I sigh. "You just need to figure it out for yourself first." I smile at her and she nods her head.

"Thanks Stace. You're a good friend."

"Just a good one?" I say playfully.

"The best."

"That's better." We both laugh and then turn our attention to the film. It's about three quarters of the way through. We watch the rest in silence. The end of the film always chokes me. The love that they have for each other makes me hope that love like theirs isn't just in films, or written in books. It's the kind of love that I hope that Jake and I will always have. Unconditional.

"Want to watch another one?" Lydia asks, disrupting my thoughts.

"Sure." I don't really, but I don't want to be rude. She starts to flick through the movie channels and stumbles across our all-time favourite.

"Dirty Dancing. Oh yes," she says as she snuggles further into the sofa.

"I'm just going to go and check on Jake quickly," I say. It may be my all-time favourite film, but my all-time favourite man is upstairs and I want to get him back for his panty dropping antics earlier.

"Uh huh," Lydia mumbles, already engrossed by the sight of Patrick Swayze on the screen. I leave the lounge and make my way to Jake's office. As I stand in the door way, I see that he is on the phone. I study him for a few moments, revelling in the fact that he's mine. He could have his pick of women, but he chose me. *Me!* I smile and tap lightly on the door. His eyes shoot up and lock with mine, his face breaking into a grin. He motions for me to come in. I walk over to his desk, his eyes never leaving mine, and I perch on the edge so that I am facing him. He's still on the phone, and I decide that I will use this moment to push his buttons. I lower myself, so that I am kneeling in front of him. I move my hands to the zip on his trousers and I slowly pull it down. I undo the button and then snake my hand into his boxers, enjoying the feel of how hard he is when I haven't even done anything yet. I make him feel like this, and that is beyond thrilling. He is trying to speak to whoever is on the other end of the phone, managing to keep his voice even, until the moment that I pull his cock out of his boxers and place my lips over the tip. I hear the intake of his breath, and his words become staggered. I look up at him from underneath my lashes, and his expression is one that makes my knickers wet with desire. I start my movements slow and tantalising. He is desperately trying to keep control, but he is failing. I chuckle around his length and then increase the pressure, sucking harder. Jake lets out a gasp.

"I have to go. I'll call you back," he says, his tone dominating. He chucks the phone on the desk and then places his hands on either side of my head. I work him until he is reaching his peak. The shallowness and the speed of his breathing, and the low groan all signal that he is close. His hands have moved to grip the arms of his chair. Just when I know that he is about to explode with pleasure, I pull away, freeing him from my mouth. His eyes are still closed as I stand up and quickly make my way to the other side of the desk. When his eyes open, he looks dazed, dumbfounded. I smirk and stand there with my arms folded, waiting to see what his next move will be.

"Uh, why are you all the way over there?" he asks, his expression one of complete confusion.

"It's not nice being left all hot and bothered, is it?" I raise one eyebrow at him, turn on my heel, and exit the room. I giggle to myself at the look on his face. Maybe he will think twice before he tries to leave me high and dry again.

Chapter Eight.

Stacey.

I wake up to the sound of Lydia snoring. I groggily open my eyes and see that she is sprawled out on the sofa. We must have both fallen asleep whilst watching the television last night. I stretch my arms above my head and yawn. I need a cup of coffee. I move off of the part of the sofa that Lydia hasn't occupied and I quietly start to make my way to the kitchen. I don't want to wake Lydia as she needs her rest, especially after the events that transpired yesterday. I shut the lounge door behind me and walk through to the kitchen. The sight of Jake's back greets me, his shirt slightly stretched across his broad shoulders. I shiver in delight. I make my way over to him, put my arms around him from behind, and place my lips by his ear.

"Good morning handsome," I purr. He puts down the cup of coffee that he is holding and turns his head to look at me.

"Good morning." His reply is a little abrupt and I get the feeling that he is pissed off with me about last night. I place a light kiss on his lips and then I go to make myself a coffee. I smile to myself as I hum along to the radio that Jake has playing in the background. He doesn't say another word, but I can feel his gaze bore into my back. I decide to take my coffee upstairs with me whilst I get ready for the day ahead. I am hoping that it will just be a straight forward day, but my life of late is anything but straight forward so I don't get my hopes up too much. I smile at Jake as I make my way out of the kitchen and upstairs to our bedroom. I put my coffee down on the bedside table and go to the ensuite. I take a quick shower, reasoning that my coffee will be cool enough to drink by the time that I have finished. I wash quickly, get out and wrap myself in a towel. I am picking out my clothes to wear for the day, when Jake walks in. As I pick out a pair of tailored grey trousers and black, fitted, shirt to wear, I watch him out of the corner of my eye. He stands there, with his hands in his trouser pockets, looking like a god. I fight the urge to go to him as I select my underwear to put on. I choose a red lace bra and matching thong, knowing that Jake loves to see me in the colour red. I saunter past him, faking ignorance of him as I return to the ensuite. I close the door behind me, smirking and start to dry myself off with the towel. The smirk is soon wiped from my face though, as Jake bursts through the door, making me drop the towel in shock. *Damn him for not having a lock on this door.*

"Do you mind?" I say, as I watch his eyes rake over my naked body. "I am trying to get dressed." My nipples harden from his penetrating stare. In a flash, he comes towards me and has me pinned against the wall. The heat in Jake's eyes is enough to make me weak at the knees, but I somehow manage to contain my excitement from his body being pressed up against mine. I know that he is looking for a bit of payback after I failed to finish him off last night. I maintain eye contact with him, all the while, fighting the urge to kiss his full, inviting lips. His head swoops down and he trails kisses from my neck, up to my cheek. I resist the urge to close my eyes from desire. With my arms pinned above my head, and Jake's body pressing against mine, I am unable to move. Not that I really want to move. I can think of nothing better than having Jake pressed up against me. His lips trail from my cheek and down to my breasts, where he flicks each nipple in turn with his tongue. I let out an involuntary moan as he continues his delicious assault of my nipples. He shuffles my hands slightly so that he is pinning them to the wall using just one of his hands rather than both. His, now free hand, comes down and trails across my stomach. He licks his way back up to my neck and his hand fondles one of my breasts. My breathing becomes staggered as my senses heighten. The combination of his mouth on me, and his tweaking of my nipple, causes me to cry out in pleasure. I feel his lips pull into a smile against my skin. His hand traces its way down to my sex, which is already wet and ready for him. He strokes me and my body shudders.

"Your body betrays you my love," he whispers in my ear, causing my skin to heat from his breath. I look at him and see the cheeky smile spread across his face. He knows that I can't deny him. He knows that I lose all sense of reason when he touches me. I know that he is about to leave me wanting more, just like I did to him last night. Suddenly, my idea for payback doesn't seem like it was a very good one.

"Ass," I whisper, making him chuckle deep in his throat.

"Yours will be mine later," he says as he cocks an eyebrow, releases me, and walks out of the ensuite. That is the second time, in less than twenty-four hours, that he has got me all hot and bothered and then just left me hanging. Bastard. It takes me a few moments to regain any sort of composure. Once I do, I get myself dressed and then head into the bedroom. I style my hair so that it is poker straight. *I need to think of a way to get Jake back for his little performance just now. There is no way that he is getting away with it again.* I grab my phone off of the bedside table and dial Martin's number.

"Hey baby girl. What's shaking?" he says as he answers after only two rings.

"I need your assistance with a sexual revenge plan." I get straight to the point.

"Lunch break at one o clock."

"Great. I'll come to your office and I will bring lunch."

"Excellent. Oh, how I do love a good bit of sexual revenge," Martin says, chuckling down the phone. I smile as an idea starts to form in my head already. Mr Jake Waters is going to wish that he had never started this game with me.

Chapter Nine.

Stacey.

I arrive at Waters Industries just after half past twelve, after dropping Lydia back at her flat. I spent all morning trying to keep her mind occupied, but it was no good. She is still worried about what to do. I told her that I would phone her later, but she just seemed to be consumed by her own thoughts. I enter the lobby and walk straight to the lifts. I'm too early to meet Martin for his lunch break, but that's okay as I need to see Jake first. I enter the lift, when it opens, and I push the button for the floor that houses Jake's office. I'm alone in the lift, so I admire my appearance in the mirrored walls. I decided against wearing the grey trousers and black shirt, and opted for something sexier. I'm wearing my fishnet tights, tight black pencil dress and my red stilettos. I left my hair down, seeing as I straightened it earlier, and I have teamed my ensemble with a sleek, black briefcase. The professional, but sexy vibe, has never been more appropriate. My make-up is more striking than usual. I have gone for the smokey eye effect and a dark shade of red lipstick that will have Jake eating out of the palm of my hand. The lift opens and I exit, making a beeline for Jake's office. I stop in front of Valerie's desk and she looks up at me and smiles.

"Oh, hello dear," she greets me. She really is a lovely woman and always has a welcoming smile on her face. "Mr Waters is just finishing up a meeting. Shall I inform him that you are here?"

"Yes please Valerie," I reply sweetly. I take a seat outside his office and wait. I listen to Valerie buzz through to Jake, and within a minute, a couple of men walk out of his office. I have my legs crossed in front of me and the men eye me appreciatively. I smile back at them so as not to appear rude, when I see Jake stood in his office doorway, scowling at me. I know that he isn't happy that the men were looking at me in a hungry manner. I keep the smile plastered on my face as I approach him, swaying my hips as I move. I squeeze past him and enter his office, making my way to his desk.

"No interruptions," I hear Jake say to Valerie. I put my briefcase on his desk and then I turn around and lean against the edge of the desk. Jake clicks the office door shut and puts his hands in his trouser pockets. I love it when he does that, it makes him look so powerful and dominant. He stalks towards me and I start to get a flutter in my stomach. *Good grief, he is so hot. Will I ever tire of looking at him?* He stops a couple of feet in front of me and raises his eyebrows in question.

"Hi baby," I purr at him. I know that he will be wondering why I am not in a bad mood from him leaving me in the ensuite this morning.

"Hi." His reply is short as his eyes roam my body from top to toe. His eyes twinkle as he drinks in my appearance, signalling that this was definitely the right choice of clothing to wear. I clear my throat to get his attention. His gaze snaps back to mine, and I would like nothing more than to make love to him on this desk, but I have a plan to stick to.

"I can't stay long as I'm meeting Martin for lunch." I need to stay focussed and keep my head in the game for this to work.

"You mean, you haven't come to have lunch with me?"

"No, afraid not." He looks disappointed, but I brush it off. I push myself off of the desk and saunter to him, placing my hands on his firm, toned chest. "I just wanted to say that, I'm sorry for leaving you high and dry last night. I feel bad and I was hoping that we could make up for it tonight?"

"Hmmm, and what exactly did you have in mind?" he asks. I run my hands up his chest and link them around his neck, bringing his lips down to mine. I kiss him slowly, and I move one of my hands down to his crotch.

"I think that you can guess, but let me spell it out for you. I want this," I squeeze his crotch gently to indicate what I am talking about, "inside me. I want these," I take my other hand and brush my thumb over his lips, "all over me. I want every inch of my body to be worshipped by you." I plant another kiss on his lips and he groans deep in the back of his throat. "And I want this," I grab one of his hands and place it on my ass, "to be broken in by you." That does it, I am pushed back onto the desk and laid down, Jake's body covering mine. His lips crash down onto mine. My hands grab Jake's hair, pulling gently. My plan is working. He is putty in my hands. I mentally give myself a high five. The buzzer on Jake's desk rings and Valerie's voice informs us that Jake's one o clock meeting has arrived early, even though he told her not to interrupt us. I'm guessing that the meeting is important though for Valerie to go against Jake's orders. Jake breaks our kiss and grunts in frustration. He stands up, pulling me with him.

"Fucking meetings," he curses as he straightens out his jacket. "You're a bad girl Miss Paris."

"I prefer the term dirty, but I suppose bad is okay," I tease.

"How am I meant to concentrate on my meeting now?"

"I'm sure you'll manage," I whisper in his ear. I stand tall and pick my briefcase up, off of the desk. "See you at home handsome." I side step him and walk to his office door. I turn my head before I open the door, and I find Jake transfixed on me, just as I knew he would be.

"I'm going to ruin you Miss Paris."

"That's what I'm counting on." Inside I am doing a little victory dance at how well this part of my plan has gone.

"Before you go, could you try and do me a favour?" Jake asks.

"Sure, what is it?"

"Can you try not to give any of my business associates a heart attack on the way out. That outfit is far too sexy for you to be wearing out in public." I smile at him, give him a wink and I open the door. I walk out of his office feeling more than satisfied with myself. I wave goodbye to Valerie and I ignore the guy that is currently waiting to see Jake. I return to the lifts and wait for one to become available. When one does, I press the button for Martin's floor and I make my way to his office. I get to Martin's office and I knock on the door. I don't want to barge in if he is busy.

"Come in," I hear him shout. I open the door and I get a wolf whistle off of him as I walk in. "Hey baby girl."

"Hi Mart," I reply, taking a seat on the chair opposite him.

"I take it by the way you are dressed, that the sexual revenge plan is in full swing?" he asks, one eyebrow raised.

"It is indeed."

"You don't waste any time do you?"

"Nope."

"Did you bring lunch?" I roll my eyes at him and place my briefcase on my lap, clicking it open. I pull out two large trays of sushi and place them in front of Martin. "OMG. I fucking love you. You do know how to spoil me," Martin says. He doesn't waste any time in opening up one of the trays and shoving some salmon into his mouth. "Mmmm, mmmm, mmmm. Delish."

"Okay, calm down there. It's just sushi." I laugh as I take a piece of salmon for myself. I know that sushi is Martin's favourite food, but I didn't expect him to almost orgasm over eating it. I pull two bottles of iced tea out of my briefcase, and hand one to Martin.

"Ah, I love you even more." Martin opens his bottle and takes a few swigs. "Mmmm. Heaven."

"Can we stop climaxing over the food and drink choices now please?" I say, playfully.

"Sorry." He doesn't look sorry.

"So, how has your first week here been?" I ask, after finishing my mouthful of food.

"It's fabulous darling. I have so many events to plan, and I love the atmosphere in this place. I owe you one baby girl. If it weren't for you, I would still be working for that douche-bag Charles."

"No problem. I'm glad that you like it here." I'm so pleased that Jake hired Martin. I think he is really going to appreciate having Martin on his payroll.

"Now, stop stalling, and tell me about this plan of yours that you have already put into action." I chuckle to myself and take a sip of my drink. Martin places his hands under his chin, resting his head on his palms, waiting for me to fill him in. I quickly tell him about what happened last night, and this morning, and then I finish off with what I just did in Jake's office. Martin gasps. "Stacey Paris, I never had you down as such a hussy. I love it!" I laugh at his reaction.

"What I really need now though, is a pair of handcuffs." Martin splutters, and bits of sushi fly across his desk. "Ewww," I squeal as I push my chair back slightly.

"Sorry," he says, once he has swallowed the remainder of his food. I sit there and patiently wait for him to regain his composure. "It takes a lot to shock me, and I certainly never had you down as a handcuff kind of girl." I shrug my shoulders at him.

"What can I say? Jake brings out my naughty side." Martin laughs and opens one of his desk drawers. He pulls out a pair of handcuffs, still in their packaging, and places them on the desk. My mouth drops open.

"Martin," I say slowly. "Do I even want to know why you have a pair of handcuffs, in your desk drawer, at work?"

"You never know when an opportunity may present itself," he answers, with no shame. "You need to be prepared darling." He is completely unfazed by my shock. "As you can see, I am yet to use them." I scoff and he pushes the handcuffs towards me. I pick them up and put them in my briefcase.

"Uh, thanks," I say, still shocked that he produced the very item that I needed.

"No worries. My gift to you." He bursts out laughing and I join in with him. Tonight is certainly going to be a night that Jake will remember forever.

Chapter Ten.

Stacey.

I leave Martin's office, once his lunch break has ended, and I head to the lifts. The doors ping open and I falter as I enter the lift. Jake is stood there, by himself, looking devilishly handsome. *How any of the women working here get any work done is beyond me. I would be rendered useless every time that Jake was in sight.* I stand beside him and face the lift doors. I see that Jake is travelling to the ground floor, so there is no need for me to push the button. My heart rate speeds up as the lift doors close. We stand there, staring at each other in the mirrored walls.

"A pleasure to see you again Miss Paris." I love the way he says my name, and I smile at him.

"You too Mr Waters."

"If only there weren't any camera's in here." I raise my eyebrow in question. "If there weren't, then you would be up against the wall right now, gasping for breath," he says, calmly. I intake a sharp breath and keep my eyes fixed on him. I can feel the heat rushing up my body. The lift stops, and the doors open on the ground floor. We both stride out and into the lobby, Jake placing his hand at the bottom of my spine. I see a few envious looks from some of the female staff, but I ignore them. We exit the building and I see Eric is waiting outside, with the limo.

"Hi Eric," I say, giving him a wave.

"Miss Stacey," Eric replies, with a nod of his head. I turn to Jake and put my hand on his chest to stop him from walking any further.

"You know," I whisper in his ear, "It would have been *you* gasping for breath in that lift." Jake raises his eyebrows. "I'll see you later handsome." I place a quick kiss on his cheek as I walk in the direction of the car park.

"Stacey," I hear Jake call my name. I stop and turn my head to look at him. He stands there with a sexy as hell glint in his eye. "I'll be home at five. You better be ready for me."

"Oh I will be, don't you worry about that." He grins and I turn back around and carry on walking. He really won't be expecting what I have in store for him. I reach the car park and get into my car. I drive to the mall, as I need to purchase some attire for this evening's plan. I really should be at The Den catching up on paperwork, but my sex revenge plan trumps the idea of work. I fire off a quick text to Susie telling her that I will be unavailable tonight after all. I hope she doesn't get too pissed off. I reason with myself that she enjoys filling in for me, when I am not there. I will definitely need to spend the day there tomorrow though. When I reach the mall, I park the car and head straight to the designer lingerie shop. I walk in, and there are hundreds of beautiful pieces to choose from. However, I am not just looking for something beautiful. I am looking for something that stands out and screams sexy, but classy and stunning at the same time. I make my way through the shop, perusing every item that I can see, but it isn't until I reach the back of the shop that I find what I am looking for. On the back wall, is the most gorgeous white lace bodysuit that I have ever seen. The intricate detail of the lace gives me a shiver down my spine as I picture Jake's face at seeing me in this garment. I look through the rack and locate my size. The bodysuit has a plunging neck line and pretty, small and delicate rhinestones running down the sides. I don't bother to try it on. I know that this is the perfect choice. I hurry to the counter to pay for it, and I nearly faint at the price when the sales assistant scans the barcode. I hand over my card, trying to conceal my shock at the amount. As I put my pin in the card machine, I realise how ridiculous it is that I am spending such an obscene amount of money on one item. I argue with myself that I am making good money now, and there is no better way to spend it. If I can't buy something that is definitely going to bring Jake to his knees begging, then it's a poor job. After purchasing the bodysuit, I go to the shoe shop and buy some white stilettos to complete the look that I will be going for. I have everything else that I need at home, so I return to my car and pump up the music as I drive back.

I get back to the house at half past three, leaving me an hour and a half to get ready before Jake arrives home. I run up the stairs, shower, shave and moisturise every part of my body. I decide to put my hair up, into a high ponytail, so that it doesn't cover up the top part of the bodysuit. I slip the white lace bodysuit on and assess my appearance in the mirror. I admire how the bodysuit hugs my curves and how it accentuates my breasts. I put the white stilettos on and I apply some nude make-up to finish the look. I can't wait to see the look on Jake's face when he sees me. I check the time and see that I have ten minutes left until he arrives home. I race downstairs and carry one of the chairs, from the dining table, up to the bedroom. I position the chair to the side of the bed, and I take the handcuffs out of my briefcase. I rip the packaging off of them and hide them under my pillow, on the bed, before I race to the hall way window. The limo is pulling onto the driveway and my heart starts to beat wildly. Jake gets out of the limo and my whole body shivers with excitement. He is so perfect that sometimes, I feel the need to pinch myself, just so I know that I am not dreaming. I watch him walking up the steps to the front door, and I race back to the bedroom. I take a few deep breaths as I take my white silk dressing gown off of the back of the bedroom door. I put it on and tie it around myself.

"Stacey?" I hear Jake shout out from downstairs. I check myself over in the mirror once more, and I walk to the top of the stairs.

"Up here," I call down to him. I wait as I hear him approaching. When he finally comes into view, my heart does a little flutter. His eyes peruse my attire, and he raises one eyebrow in question. I try to stop my body from shaking. I need to remain in control. "Good afternoon at work?" I ask him, innocently.

"Not too bad." He slowly starts to walk up the stairs towards me, like a predator about to strike for its prey. "And what have you been up to?" he asks as he reaches the top of the stairs. I take a few steps backwards, needing to leave some space between us. If he touches me, then my plan will go to hell.

"Oh, nothing much."

"May I ask why you are standing there looking insanely fuckable in those heels?" I smile at his comment.

"Wait and see baby. Want to follow me into the bedroom?"

"Hell yeah." I turn and walk to the bedroom, Jake following behind me. I stop when I reach the bed and whirl around so that I am facing him. He stops and looks at the chair, eyeing my suspiciously.

"What's the chair for?" he asks.

"You'll find out soon enough. Now, strip." Jake's eyes go wide at my commanding tone. I keep a straight face and hope to god that he does as I ask. After a few moments, Jake starts to remove his clothes. He keeps his eyes on me the whole time. I feel my face flush as more and more of his naked body is revealed. I struggle to regulate my breathing as he removes his boxers and stands there in all his naked glory. His body really is spectacular. I clear my throat and find my voice. "Get on the bed and lie facing upwards."

"Feeling dominant, are we?" he teases, but I can tell that he is getting turned on by my tone.

"Get on the bed Waters." I keep my voice firm, ignoring his question. He lets out a low growl and does as I ask. I keep the dressing gown on, and I sit by him on the bed. He goes to touch me but I wag my finger at him and shake my head. He, reluctantly, puts his hands back by his sides and waits to see what I am going to do next. "Arms above your head," I instruct. He complies immediately. I lean over him, placing a soft kiss on his lips as I pull out the handcuffs. I shake them in front of his face. I smirk at him and place one of the cuffs on his wrist. He watches as I hook the handcuffs around one of the wooden rails, on the headboard, and I then put the other cuff around his other wrist, locking it in place. *Well, that was easier than I expected. I thought that he would make a fuss.*

"Um, babe, I can't touch you if I'm handcuffed like this."

"Exactly." I smile, stand up off of the bed and face him. He watches me intently as I untie the belt on my dressing gown and take it off, letting it pool at my feet.

"Fuck me," he exclaims as he admires my choice of lingerie. "You look like an angel." I smile at him and I climb back onto the bed so that I am straddling him. Bringing my face down to his, I allow our lips to touch and sparks fly immediately, as they always do. He groans as I massage his tongue with mine. I can feel his cock standing to attention, and it takes all of my effort to break our kiss and pull away from him. He looks at me with a dazed expression on his face. I move off of him and stand by the side of the bed. He frowns at me, clearly annoyed that I have halted proceedings.

"Uh, what are you doing?" he asks, looking puzzled. This is the part of the plan that I have been looking forward to the most.

"Well baby, this is called payback."

"Payback?"

"Yes. Payback." I smile and wait for it to dawn on him.

"Payback for what?" Clearly, he isn't quite there yet.

"For this morning." I see that realisation hits him, and he doesn't look amused.

"Okay. I get it. Very funny. You have made your point. Now, can you please let me out of these handcuffs?"

"No."

"Why not?" He is not happy with how this little scenario is panning out.

"Because Mr Waters," I answer, sweetly. "I'm not finished with you yet." He stares at me as I start to remove my bodysuit. I make sure that I take my time as heat builds in his eyes. I slide the bodysuit down my torso and I place it to one side. I take a seat on the chair and I smile.

"Now what?" he asks me.

"Now you get to watch me whilst I pleasure myself."

"Oh, fuck no. Stace, you can't do that to me. Come on, just let me out of these handcuffs."

"No way Waters. I'm just finishing what you didn't." I bring my hand up to my neck and I slowly trail my fingers down my body, until I get to my stomach. I pause my hand, and I spread my legs wide, giving him a perfect eyeful. He looks like he is going to pass out, but in a good way. I start to move my hand down lower, and when I let my finger brush against my clit, I let out a low moan.

"Babe please," he pleads with me. "I need to touch you." I ignore him and continue to stimulate myself. My hand moves in a circular motion, allowing me to slowly build up my climax. My breathing quickens, and my eyelids grow heavy. I won't break eye contact with Jake though. The desire burning in his caramel pools is making me wet.

"Stacey, please. I'm sorry about this morning. Just, let me out of these fucking handcuffs." Jake's voice is urgent, but I refuse to answer him. I teeter closer to the edge of release.

"Oh god," I say, breathlessly. Jake grits his teeth and I see his jaw flexing. He tries pulling his hands away from the headboard, but there is no way that he will be able to free himself. I increase the speed of my finger and I use my other hand to tweak my nipple. Jake watches me, open mouthed as I reach my climax. My body convulses as I ride out my orgasm. Jake watches on as I work myself down from my release. When I am finished, he opens his mouth to speak, but stops as he watches me put my finger in my mouth. I lick my own juices from my finger and moan in approval.

"Ah, you are fucking kidding me," Jake says, his voice still sounding urgent. "Please let me out of the cuffs now Stace." I sit there, in my post orgasmic state, relishing the feel of this moment. I have never done anything like this before, and I have to say, that I loved every minute of it. I can tell that, as much as he is annoyed that he can't touch me, Jake has enjoyed my little show. I don't think that he will be leaving me hanging again anytime soon. I stand up, pick my dressing gown up off of the floor and put it on. Jake is still staring at me, and I give him a smile.

"I'm just going to go and get a drink whilst you calm down," I tell him. I can see his jaw ticking.

"Are you not going to let me out of these cuffs first?" he asks in disbelief.

"Nope." I turn on my heel and walk from the bedroom as he shouts out my name. I make my way to the kitchen and get myself a cup of coffee. Sitting at the kitchen island, I laugh to myself at how easy my plan was to pull off. I drink my coffee quickly. I might have wanted to teach him a lesson, but I actually don't want to leave him too long. He's frustrated enough as it is. I finish my drink and I head back upstairs. Jake is lying there with his eyes closed. I walk over to the bed and open my bedside drawer. Jake opens his eyes as I produce the keys that will free him.

"Have you calmed down yet?" I ask.

"Yes."

"Are you sure?"

"Yes," he sighs. "Can you just unlock the cuffs?" I move to his left wrist and I unlock the cuff. I am about to unlock the other one, but before I can, Jake's hands are grabbing me by my waist and then I am pinned underneath him on the bed. "You're a bad girl. Do you know how horny and frustrating your little performance was to watch? To not be able to touch you?"

"I have a rough idea."

"The things you do to me."

"Well, maybe next time you will think twice about keeping me waiting." I keep an innocent look plastered on my face, but let's face it, I am far from innocent here. He chuckles and I know that he has forgiven me for handcuffing him.

"Noted." He brings his lips to mine and kisses me, his movements slow and sensual. It doesn't take long for us to forget about our game-playing as we get lost in each other, setting a precedent for what the remainder of our night together will entail.

Jake.

I watch Stacey as she sleeps beside me. This woman mesmerises me. She excites me, pleases me, thrills me, but most of all she challenges me. The little performance that she put on earlier was mind-blowing. I have never experienced anything like it. I don't know what, or who, brought this woman into my life, but I thank my lucky stars that she is in it. The women I used to date, or just sleep with, just used to fall at my feet. They were boring and un-exciting. They just used to hang on my every word and hope to god that they were going to be the one to make me settle down. Stacey is nothing like that. I love how unpredictable she is, and I hope that we never lose the chemistry that we share. Stacey turns and faces the other way, giving a little moan as she does. *God, even her back is sexy.* I get out of bed and go to use the ensuite. Even after our marathon love-making, I can't sleep. I don't want to disturb Stacey, so I decide to go to my office and check some emails. Maybe doing that will help tire me out. I switch the office lamp on, turn my laptop on and take a seat on my leather swivel chair. I wait for the computer to load and then I pull up my emails. Most of the ones that I check are just to confirm business meetings, a couple of them are junk mail, and then there is one that stands out. I inwardly groan as I see my brother's name on the sender column. He only ever contacts me when he needs something, and that is usually money. I open the email, figuring that the quicker I read it, the quicker I find out what the hell he wants.

Hey bro,

I know that we haven't spoken for a while, but I thought that I would let you know that I am back in the area. Things didn't work out in America. I've been back a few weeks and was hoping that we could catch up? You are my big brother after all. Hit me up via email and we can arrange a day and time.

Laters,

Brad.

Oh fuck. He's back? Why is he back? I drop my head in my hands as I feel the beginning of a headache coming on. I'm not exactly close to my brother. His top priority in life is chasing after some skirt, normally resulting in him getting himself into stupid situations. Of course, I usually have to bail him out of whatever situation he has got himself into. I find his behaviour embarrassing. I just wish he would grow up and act his age. He's thirty-one so there isn't a big age gap between us. We used to be close when we were younger, but as we got older, we drifted apart. I became a serious businessman and I think he resented me. I could never understand why though, seeing as he has a decent career himself. He is a general practitioner, and for all I know, he may have retrained to become a surgeon or something. Brad moving to America was a blessing. It meant that I wouldn't have to worry about what he got up to next. It's a bit like the saying, out of sight, out of mind. I haven't heard anything from him for two years. The day he left for America was the day that I thought that he was out of my life for good. *Fuck, this means that I am going to have to tell Stacey more about him.* That is a thought that I do not welcome. She knows limited information about Brad, and I wanted to keep it that way. Brad is a massive flirt and he won't care about the fact that Stacy is my girlfriend, if he ever meets her. I should know, he has form. Brad doesn't care who gets hurt, as long as he gets what he wants. He used to try and steal any girl off of me when we were younger. As we drifted apart, he seemed to want to have anything that was remotely linked to me. He succeeded in stealing a couple of girls off of me. Luckily, they never meant anything to me. What irritated me was the way Brad treated me. I am his brother, and he should have just been happy for me. But no, he was incapable of doing that. There is absolutely no fucking way that I will let him take Stacey away from me. She is mine. I close down the email and decide to deal with it at a later date. I rub my temples, trying to soothe away the impending headache.

"Babe?" My thoughts are interrupted by my gorgeous girlfriend standing in the door way, naked. "What are you doing?"

"I couldn't sleep, so I was just checking some emails."

"Oh. You okay?" she rubs her sleepy eyes and stifles a yawn.

"Yeah. I'm fine." I smile at her to reassure her that there is nothing wrong. I don't want to talk about Brad now.

"Well, in that case, are you coming back to bed? I could do with a reminder of our earlier encounter." She cocks one eyebrow at me. *Fucking hell, she is outrageous.*

"Already?" I ask in disbelief, not that I will ever complain about her wanting to fuck me. She nods her head at me, and that is all the persuading that I need. I turn off the computer and the light, and walk towards her. When I get to her, I grab her around the waist and lift her up. She wraps her legs around me and I can feel her wetness against my bare stomach. I place a kiss on her nose and carry her back to our bedroom. *Oh yes Waters, this girl is definitely a keeper.*

Chapter Eleven.

Stacey.

Jake has left by the time that I wake up. I stretch across the bed and my arm brushes against his pillow. I turn my head as I feel something on there, and I see that he has left a note for me. I pick it up eagerly.

I left you to sleep after all the exertion last night. Rematch later? Call me when you wake up. I love you. Jake x x x

I smile at his note. His personality is just perfect. He's loving and sweet, as well as being powerful. I grab my phone from the bedside table and call him. It goes straight to answerphone. *Damn, he must be in a meeting.* I scroll through the contacts on my phone and call Lydia instead.

"Hi babes," she says as she answers the phone.

"Morning Lyd. I just wanted to see how you were feeling this morning?"

"I'm good. Actually, I'm great. I'm seeing Paul, after work tonight, and I'm going to tell him everything."

"Really?" I can't hide the shock in my voice. I wanted her to tell Paul, but I thought that it may have taken longer than a couple of days for her to conclude that telling him was the only option that she actually had.

"I'm guessing that you didn't expect me to be saying that," she says as she chuckles down the phone. At least she isn't annoyed by my obvious shock. "I figured that, if I want to build a future with him, then I have to be honest with him. Well, that's if there even will be a future with him after tonight."

"I'm sure it will be fine. Paul's a good guy Lyd."

"I know." As she answers her voice is quiet and I know that she deeply regrets ever meeting that Callum guy.

"If you need me at any point, promise that you will call me."

"Of course I will. And, Stace?" she pauses and I can hear her voice crack a little as she says my name.

"Yeah?" I prompt her.

"Thanks for not telling Jake. I know that you don't like keeping stuff from him. And, thank you for being there for me after everything." I know what she is referring to. I know that she still feels bad about the things that she said to me during her bad patch. As far as I am concerned though, it is in the past, and that is where it is staying. I hold no malice against her.

"That's what friends are for Lyd." I have nothing but love for this girl.

"I know, but you have done more for me than anyone else ever has. Even if I don't always realise that." I smile at her words. "Oh, and I bumped into Martin yesterday. He told me to ask you about a pair of handcuffs." I can hear the mischief in her voice.

"Uh....." I'm lost for words. Lydia starts to laugh.

"I want details when I next see you missy. There is no way that I am letting you keep that secret to yourself. Anyway, I best go. Nick is waiting to take me out for breakfast. Talk to you later babes."

"Bye Lyd." I hang up feeling relieved that I didn't have to tell her all about my sexual revenge plan over the phone. I will be having words with Martin when I next speak to him. He's got such a big mouth sometimes. I get out of bed and get showered and dressed. I really need to get to The Den and do some bloody work.

Jake.

Fucking hell, how is it only just half past ten in the morning? My day has already gone to shit and I have hours left yet. The accounting department are really trying my patience. I dropped the idea of buying Charles Montpellior's business when most of his clients left him and came to my company anyway. The only problem is, my accounting staff are snowed under and clients are being kept waiting. I pride myself on dealing with issues quickly and efficiently, so I need to figure out a plan of action on how to handle all of the extra work. The ideal solution is to employ more staff. I could leave it to the accounting manager to deal with, but I like to make the final decisions on who I hire and fire. Trouble is, I don't have a free day in my diary for weeks. I know that I need to relinquish some control, but after successfully building up my business alone, it's hard to let others take over. I grab my phone out of my desk drawer and switch it on. I need a distraction, and there is only one distraction that will be sufficient, and that is Stacey. The screen lights up and I am notified that I have a missed call from her. I call her back, hoping that she can lighten my shitty mood. The phone rings and rings and then goes to answerphone. I sigh and hang up. The buzzer on my desk goes, signalling that Valerie needs to speak to me.

"What is it Valerie?" My tone is harsher than intended.

"I'm sorry sir, I know that you are very busy, but there is a gentleman here that says he needs to see you, urgently."

"You need to be a little bit more specific Valerie. There are plenty of people who want to see me. What's his name?" I ask, irritation evident in my tone.

"He won't say sir. I have tried to tell him that you have no free time, but he says that he will wait all day if he has to." She sounds a little nervous answering me.

"Okay. Go ahead and send, whoever it is in." I sigh and keep my eyes fixed on my office door. I want to see who the hell needs to interrupt my time so badly. As the door opens and the guy in question comes into view, I immediately wish that I hadn't told her to send him on in. I have a feeling that my morning is about to get a whole lot worse.

"Hey, my man," says Brad as he confidently strides into the room. He takes a seat in the chair on the other side of my desk and sits back, looking relaxed and comfortable. "It's been a long time brother." His familiarity immediately pisses me off.

"Yes, it has. So, what trouble have you got yourself into now?" I decide to get straight to the point of why he is here. Brad makes a big show of pretending to be offended by my comment.

"Now what makes you think that I would be in trouble?" His hand goes over his heart as if he is wounded. I roll my eyes at how dramatic he can be. He definitely missed his calling to be an actor.

"Brad, the only reason that you ever come to see me is if you are in trouble. I haven't seen, or heard, from you in two years, and here you are, casually waltzing in here as if we spoke just yesterday. Forgive me for side stepping all of your usual bullshit and getting straight to the point."

"I came here to catch up with my bro. That's all. No ulterior motive, I swear." He holds his hands up in surrender. I raise my eyebrows at him. I don't believe him for one second.

"Uh huh." I can't be bothered to play along with his stupid games, so I decide to be blunt. "Look Brad, I'm busy. If this is just a social call, then it's going to have to be done some other time."

"Wow, things really don't change do they? Still the boring, hard-nosed boss man that you always were."

"A little ambition never hurt anyone." I refuse to rise to his taunts.

"I agree, but you are obsessed by it. Why don't you just relax and take a chill pill once in a while. There's more to life than work Jake." We have, pretty much, the same conversation every time that we see each other. I smirk at the fact that he doesn't know how much fun I actually do have in my private life. "You're not still pissed with me over Tara Benson, are you?" he asks and I laugh at his ridiculous question.

"Grow up Brad. I couldn't give a shit about you and Tara." Tara is the girl that he took to America with him. The girl that I slept with once before she realised that I wasn't going to settle down with her. Brad swooped in and charmed her, and she fell for whatever crap he fed her. If he thinks that I am pissed off by it, then he is sadly mistaken.

"Just checking."

"Still as cocky as ever."

"The ladies love it," Brad replies, grinning. "Listen bro, why don't we catch up over a few beers? Say, tonight? I can't imagine that you have anything exciting planned."

"I'm busy tonight." My mobile phone chooses this moment to start ringing. I look to the screen and see Stacey's face lit up, telling me that she is the one calling me. I smile and am about to answer the phone, when I stop myself. I don't want Brad eavesdropping on my conversation with her. I will phone her back when he has fucked off and left me alone. I hear him wolf whistle as he hovers over my desk. His eyes are on my phone.

"Wow. Nice work bro. She is hot." I feel my blood boil at his comment.

"Why are you still here Brad?" I can't hide the anger in my voice.

"Whoa, calm down. What's your problem?" he asks me.

"I have already told you that I don't have the fucking time for a social call. Either you tell me what you really want, or you get the fuck out of my office." I know that I am being a little unreasonable, but I can't help it. The thought of him being attracted to Stacey riles me. She is my whole fucking life. He is not going to charm her and steal her away from me. Brad stands up, giving me a wary look.

"Look bro, I didn't come here with an agenda. I simply came because I figured that we could try and forge some sort of relationship again. I know that I have been an asshole in the past, but I have changed. I'm a different person now Jake." I scoff which interrupts his little speech. He shakes his head and turns, walking towards the door. He places his hand on the door handle and then turns back around to face me. "If you want to talk like adults at some point, then feel free to call me. I sent you an email earlier with my number on." With that, he opens the door and leaves, slamming the door behind him.

"Fuck it," I say out loud to myself. I rub my temples and will the impending migraine to piss off. *Maybe he's right? Maybe I do need to chill out a bit more?* However, deep down, I know that it is just his presence that has me feeling like this. He really is a pain in my ass. I pick my phone up to call Stacey back. I need to speak to her. She will be able to calm me down. It rings and goes to answerphone again. *Bollocks.* I chuck my phone onto the desk and sit back in my chair. I need to get out of here and clear my head.

Chapter Twelve.

Stacey.

I arrive home just after five o clock. It has been a long day. I have been sorting out paperwork all day at The Den, and now I have to get changed, ready to go back in an hour and start the evening shift. All I really want to do is relax, with Jake, but I can't ask Susie to cover for me again. It wouldn't be fair to her. Plus, I need to show that I am an active member of the team, even if I am the boss. I run upstairs and go straight to my mobile phone, which I left on the bedside table when I left home this morning. I put my bag on the bed and sit on the edge. Looking at my phone, I see that I have a couple of texts from Jake, and a shit load of missed calls. I sigh and decide to read the messages before I call him back.

Hey baby, we seem to keep missing each other today. I have no more meetings now, so call when you can. Love you. Jake x x x

This is ridiculous, I miss your voice. Call me asap. Jake x x x

I smile at his eagerness to speak to me. It's exactly the same for me when I haven't spoken to him for a while. I hope that this feeling never fades. I open the last message from him, and my smile soon disappears as I read the words.

How the fuck could you do this to me? Don't look for me. I don't want to see you right now.

Huh? Is this message meant for me? I call Jake's phone but it goes straight to answerphone. I call his office next, but there is no answer. I even try to call Eric, but his phone goes to answerphone too. *What the hell?* I start to panic at the fact that I can't get hold of him. I take off my shoes and rack my brains for a reasonable explanation for his message. I change out of my skirt and shirt combo, and I put on my skinny jeans and a fitted white t-shirt. I put on my black shoe boots and pick my bag up off of the bed. With my phone in hand, I try to ring Jake again, but it still goes to answerphone. I make my way downstairs, still feeling confused by Jake's last message. As I enter the kitchen though, I freeze. My eyes widen as I stare at the leaflets that litter the kitchen island.

"Oh no," I say out loud. I walk slowly over to the island, and my heart starts to beat faster. My eyes scan the leaflets and it dawns on me what Jake's message was about. Panic starts to course through me at the sight of the abortion leaflets that Jake has clearly seen. My breathing starts to speed up as I realise how stupid I have been. I should have thrown the leaflets away. The bag that I had put them in is on the floor, with all the contents spilled out. I can only assume that Jake knocked it over and the leaflets fell out. *Fuck!* I can also only assume that Jake thinks that these leaflets belong to me. *Of course he thinks that they belong to you Stacey. They were in your fucking bag.* I let out a sound of rage. I need to find him. God knows what is going on in his head right now. I pick up the leaflets, tear them into pieces and throw them in the bin. Nausea overwhelms me and I grab the edge of the counter to steady myself. *Where would he have gone? His office? Paul's house?* I rack my brains, but ultimately, he could be anywhere. I am about to try and phone him again, praying that his phone has miraculously switched on, when the screen lights up, making me jump. Lydia's name is across the screen and I hurriedly answer, needing to speak to someone.

"Lyd, thank god you called………"

"Babes, you need to get your ass to The Den. *Now.*" She says, cutting me off mid-sentence. I don't fail to notice the urgency in her voice.

"What's going on?" I ask, suddenly getting a bad feeling settling deep in the pit of my stomach.

"Jake's here, and he's not alone." My heart fills with dread at her words. I slowly sit on the stool as my knees go weak.

"What do you mean he's not alone?" I whisper. I speak so quietly that I am surprised that she can hear me.

"Just get down here. I'll be waiting at the back door for you."

"Okay." I hang up the phone and take in what she has said. She obviously doesn't want to tell me over the phone, and that just makes me more nervous about what I might see when I get there. A few minutes go past before I feel like I can stand. When I do, I take my phone and handbag, and I walk into the hall way. As I reach the front door, I pick up my keys and leave the house, locking the door behind me. I feel like I am in a daze as I get in my car and start to drive to The Den. It's like I'm on autopilot as I pull into The Den car park. Lydia is waiting by the back door, and when she sees me, she comes walking over. I park the car and get out. The look on her face is grim and I know that I am not going to like what I am about to see. My whole body starts to shake as Lydia stops in front of my car.

"Where is he?" I say in a firm tone. I sound a lot more confident than I feel right now.

"He's sat at one of the tables at the back of the dancefloor, in the corner. Stace………" I don't hear anything else she says as I march through the back door and head straight for the main room. As I enter the main room, my eyes scan the tables at the back. My gaze zones in on Jake straight away. He is sat there with some young woman draped all over him. She is sat on his lap and she's whispering something in his ear. I feel my blood boil and my hands curl into fists at my sides. I know that there is no way that I am going to remain calm for the scene that will unfold in the next few moments. I feel Lydia put her hand on my arm, but I shrug her off. I am in a state of shock at the sight of Jake with another woman. Before I can think about my how I am going to approach this scenario, I am walking over to him. As I get nearer to the table, Jake's eyes lock with mine. I can see hurt and anger clouding his vision, but I am sure that mine reflect the same feelings. I reach the table and stand there with my hands on my hips. I don't think that I have ever been so mad with someone in my entire life. I am physically shaking with anger.

"What the fuck are you doing?" I shout at him. I don't give a shit if other people hear me. Right now, all that exists is my idiot boyfriend, and the tart that is currently sat on his lap. The woman's head whips round so fast that I am surprised that she doesn't give herself whiplash. The smile quickly disappears from her face and her eyes widen with surprise. Jake's arm is around her waist, and it takes all of my willpower not to rip his arm off of her and physically drag her from his lap. He takes a sip of his drink, never removing his gaze from mine. It feels like I have been stood here forever waiting for him to answer me, but in reality, it must only be a few seconds.

"Stacey, this is Gemma," he says as he points to the woman on his lap. I don't fail to notice that his eyes are glazed over, indicating that he has had more than a few drinks. My eyes narrow on him before I divert my attention to this Gemma woman. When my eyes connect with hers, she looks like she is going to have a panic attack.

"Um...... hi," she mumbles, her voice irritating me instantly. I am not really sure what point Jake is trying to make here. I just need to get that woman off of him.

"Hi Gemma," I say a little bit too sweetly. I smile at her, which she returns warily, before I go in for the kill. "Let me give you a piece of advice." I lean forward so that my hands are resting on the table, allowing me to be eye level with her. She arches herself back a little, clearly uncomfortable. "The image of you sat on my boyfriend's lap is pissing me off, which I am sure that you can understand. So, here is what I think you should do." Her eyes widen some more and she quickly looks to Jake before looking back at me. His gaze hasn't left me the entire time. "Get up and walk away before I really lose my cool, and before I give you the ass kicking of a lifetime." I sound evil. I almost don't recognise my own voice. I know that Jake has been the one to create this situation, but my focus is just on getting her to leave. I see her gulp and look back to Jake.

"You have a girlfriend?" she asks him.

"I did have." His answer stings me. He doesn't look at her when he answers, his eyes remain on me. His deep caramel pools that have always captured me are now devoid of any warmth.

"Oh my god," she says as she scrambles off of his lap. "I am so sorry," she says to me. "I didn't know."

"Forget it. Now, run along." She scurries away as fast as she can. Out of the corner of my eye, I can see that Lydia is standing off to the side, clearly wary of how this situation will play out. I return my eyes to Jake. His body radiates anger.

"Now that your little plaything has gone, are you going to tell me what the fuck you think you are playing at?" I snarl at him and he scoffs.

"Me? What am I playing at? You're the one with the fucking abortion leaflets Stace, so why don't you tell me what the fuck *you* are playing at?" His tone is harsh and I hear Lydia gasp.

"They're not mine Jake."

"Oh please, don't give me that bullshit. They were in your bag Stacey. Why the fuck would you have them if they weren't yours?" He downs the rest of his drink and slams the glass on the table. "Do you know how it feels to find something like that? Fucking heart wrenching, that's how."

"They are not mine," I say again, this time through gritted teeth.

"Liar," Jake spits at me.

"Jake. They're not Stacey's," I hear Lydia say. I push myself off of the table and turn to face her. Paul has emerged from somewhere and is now standing by Lydia.

"Don't Lyd," I warn her. I try to plead with her using my eyes, but she just looks at me and places her hand on my arm. She nods at me and I see that she has unshed tears in her eyes.

"No Lydia, don't try to cover for her," Jake snarls. "It's better that I find out now what a heartless bitch she is, rather than find out further down the line." It takes all of my control not to turn around and slap him across his face. Lydia steps around me and starts to speak.

"Those leaflets are mine Jake." Jake blinks a few times and I turn to see that Paul is frowning at Lydia. I could throttle Jake for this. "Stacey came with me to a doctor's appointment the other day to confirm that I am pregnant. I was a bit of a mess in the doctor's, so Stacey took the leaflets for me. I forgot that she had them to be honest. That's why I stayed at your place the other night. I didn't want to go back to the flat and Stacey said that I was welcome to come and stay at yours. I asked Stacey not to tell you anything until I had figured out what I was going to do." I see Lydia's body start to shake slightly, and I know that it is taking all of her courage to admit to this, especially with Paul listening. Jake's expression changes to shock whilst Paul looks completely blown away by Lydia's announcement.

"You didn't have to do that Lyd," I say to her.

"Yes I did." She smiles at me and then turns to Paul. "We need to talk," she says to him. He appears to be in a daze as he just nods his head at her.

"Use my office if you need to," I say to her.

"Thanks babes. Call me later." I smile at her as she leads Paul across the main room and out towards my office. I turn back to Jake and my smile vanishes. His eyes eventually look into mine, and I can see the shame on his face.

"Stacey, I'm so............"

“Sorry?” I cut him off before he can finish. “Save it Jake. I’m not interested in listening to some pathetic apology.” I turn on my heel, needing to get as far away from him as possible. I don’t get far as he grabs my arm and turns me around to face him. “Get your fucking hands off of me,” I shout in his face as I yank my arm from his grasp.

“Please……….”

“No Jake. I suggest that you leave me the hell alone.” I turn and run through the main room and make my way to the back door. I can hear Jake shouting my name, but all I want to do is get in my car and drive away. I make it out of the back door and am just opening my car door, when Jake comes behind me and slams the car door shut. I turn so that I am facing him, and he puts his arms either side of me, resting his palms on the car. He has effectively trapped me.

“Get away from me,” I say in a low voice.

“No. I’m not going anywhere. We need to talk.”

“No, we don’t. You’re drunk and I am way too pissed off to have a rational conversation with you right now.” I try to push his body away from me, but he doesn’t budge. I desperately try to fight the tears that are threatening to emerge. I look past him, not wanting to have any eye contact with him right now.

“Please Stace,” he says, the over powering smell of whisky on his breath is wafting over my face. “I’m sorry that I thought the worst. I just saw those leaflets and………”

"And you jumped to fucking conclusions," I finish for him.

"What was I meant to think?" he says, exasperated. I close my eyes to avoid seeing the devastation on his face. "I accidentally knocked your bag onto the floor, and the leaflets fell out. I saw them, and I just………." His voice trails off as he tries to find the words to justify his actions. "I just lost it." I open my eyes and look at him. His eyes are swimming with the pain that he is feeling right now. My heart aches for him, but I quickly shut it down. The image of that girl on his lap, his arm around her waist, makes my hands curl into fists at my sides. I grit my teeth to stop myself from saying something that I will regret. "I'm so fucking sorry babe." I swallow past the lump that has formed in my throat. I need to get away from him. I need to get some head space.

"Your words don't mean anything right now." My voice sounds cold, devoid of all emotion. "I need some time to think." It's almost like I am in a daze.

"No Stace, we need to sort this out. I can't lose you." His arms have moved and are gripping the tops of mine in desperation. I can see that he is sorry, but it may not be enough. The pain that sliced through my heart at the sight of him with another woman, is a pain that is not going to heal quickly. "Please," he pleads with me. "I love you. I made a massive fucking mistake. I should have spoken to you when I found those leaflets, I just couldn't see past the anger and the hurt that you might have been considering aborting a baby of ours." His words cause the rage that I am feeling to boil over.

"How could you ever think that I would do something like that?" I shout back at him. "How could it even entertain your thoughts that I would get rid of something that was part of both of us?" My whole body is shaking. "Do you not know me at all?"

"Of course I do."

"I beg to fucking differ Jake. How low must your opinion be of me to not only think that I would kill our baby, but also for you to let some other woman sit on your lap and touch you. Your hands were around her Jake, her lips were by your ear, whispering god knows what. What would you do if some other guy had his hands on me?" My words have an effect immediately as Jake lets out a low growl and his face contorts with fury at the thought of another man touching me. "Tell me Jake, what the fuck would you be feeling if you were me right now?" He moves his hands and runs them through his hair as he lets out a cry of rage. He turns away from me momentarily, and I take that as my chance to get the hell out of here. I quickly open the car door and get in, locking the door from the inside so that Jake can't open it. He turns around at the sound of the car door shutting and tries the handle. When he realises that I have locked it, he starts to bang on the window. I ignore him and start the car.

"Stace," he bellows through the window. All I can think about is getting away from him. Getting away from a man that I love, a man that I put my complete trust in, only for him to throw it back in my face. I reverse, Jake still by the window. "Please don't go Stace," he shouts, and I can see his eyes start to glaze over. "We can work this out." As

I stare into his handsome face, I realise that I may never be able to come back from this. I may never be able to forgive his actions.

"It's too late," I mouth through the window, and I know that he has made out the words that I have spoken. He backs away from the window and I pull out of the parking space and start to drive away. The tears that I have managed to hold back are now streaming down my face. As my eyes drift to the rear-view mirror, I see Jake on his knees, his head hanging in shame at what he has done.

Jake.

I've lost her. I have acted like a complete fucking asshole, and it has come back to bite me in the ass. She couldn't even bear to look at me. I hang my head in shame, unable to look at her car driving away. *What the fuck have I done?*

Chapter Thirteen.

Stacey.

I get back to the house and find myself standing in mine and Jake's bedroom, feeling lost and alone. The tears won't stop flowing, and it feels as though my heart is shattering into a million pieces. *How could he do that to me?* The image of that woman sat on his lap will be forever ingrained on my memory. He should have just asked me about the god damn leaflets. I thought that he knew me. I thought that I knew him. I guess I was wrong. I go to the wardrobe, on autopilot, and pull out my pink holdall. I can't stay here. I need to get away. Everything here is just a painful reminder of the life that Jake and I have together. Or maybe I should say the life that we *had* together. I throw some essentials into my holdall and leave the house. I don't leave a note. Jake can't be stupid enough to think that I would stay here now. As I make my way to the front door, I realise that I have no idea where the hell I am going to go. Lydia is busy trying to sort things out with Paul after Jake's monumental fuck up. Martin has his own relationship problems to deal with, he doesn't need me bothering him with my issues. I make my way out of the house, holdall in hand, and I sit back in my car. I try to slow my racing mind, hoping that some inspiration will hit me about what to do. My phone starts to ring which breaks my thoughts. My stomach churns, thinking that it might be Jake calling me. I brace myself and look at the screen of my phone. I almost breathe a sigh of relief when I see that it is Lydia.

"Hello," I answer, glumly.

"Babes!" She sounds relieved to hear me. "Where are you?"

"I'm just at home, sat in my car." I sound so distant. "I'm just trying to decide where to go. I can't stay here."

"Come to mine," Lydia says instantly.

"No, I can't Lyd. You have stuff to figure out with Paul. You don't need me intruding on your life."

"Don't be so fucking stupid. Get your ass round to mine now. Paul and I are fine. We have talked, and we're going to work through things." I smile at the fact that Paul is prepared to see it through with Lydia. I knew that he was a good guy. She deserves that. "You however, are not fine."

"No, I'm not," I say quietly.

"Stacey, listen to me. Paul is with Jake as we speak. Paul is trying to convince Jake to give you some space, but it's like he has lost all sense of reasoning. He's on his way to yours right now. If you don't want to see him, then you need to leave, pronto."

"Shit," I say, starting the car up.

"Come to mine and you can try to figure out what to do." I have no time to think of any other plan right now, so I take Lydia up on her offer.

"Okay. I'll be there soon."

"Okay babes." I hang up the phone and pull off of the driveway. As I pull onto the main road, I see Jake and Paul on the opposite side. Jake clocks my car straight away and I start to panic. I put my foot down as I see Jake start to run towards my car. I race past him, going faster than I normally would. I can hear him shouting my name, and the pain in his voice almost makes me stop the car. I don't though. I need to sort myself out before I can even entertain the idea of speaking to Jake. I pass the turning for Lydia's and carry on along the main road. He will expect me to go to Lydia's. I knew that all along. I never should have agreed to go to hers. My mind is a cluster-fuck of emotions as I continue to drive. My phone is ringing like crazy on the passenger seat, but I ignore it. I drive for about half an hour, when I spot a bed and breakfast on the side of the main road. I pull into the car park, which is just to the right of the building. I park the car and take a look at my phone. Lydia has tried phoning me a couple of times, and the rest of the missed calls are from Jake. I will call Lydia back later. Right now, I need to see if I can get a room at this bed and breakfast for the night. I wipe my eyes, put my phone in my pocket, and pick up my handbag. The bed and breakfast is very pretty from the outside. It is a quaint cottage that looks like it has been extended at some point. Flowers adorn the window boxes in an array of colours. I exit the car and wearily walk to the front door. I ring the doorbell and wait patiently for it to be answered. It takes a few moments, but the door is eventually opened by an older lady who has a friendly smile plastered across her face. She's very petite and must be in her late fifties. She has her grey hair pulled back into a neat bun and her blue eyes sparkle, instantly making me warm towards her.

"Good evening dear, my name is Melody. How can I help you?" her voice is quiet so I have to strain to hear her properly.

"Oh, hello. I was wondering if you might have any vacant rooms available for the night?" I ask, praying that she has.

"I do have one room left. It is a double room with an ensuite. Would you like to take a look?" Melody asks me.

"Yes please," I answer, feeling relief that my snap decision to stop here is going to pay off. Melody ushers me in and shuts the door behind me. I walk into a large foyer, which has yellow pastel coloured walls and hardwood floors. There is an oak staircase directly in front of me, and there is a cabinet to the left which appears to have a guest book on the top. Melody walks over to the cabinet and unlocks it. She takes a key off of one of the hooks and then locks the cabinet back up again.

"Follow me dear," she says as she starts walking to the staircase. I follow her, taking in the surroundings as I do. There are pictures hung on the wall all the way to the top. Each one is of beautiful countryside. As we reach the top of the stairs, Melody turns to the left and then stops outside a room which has the number five on the front. She unlocks the door and ushers me in. When I enter the room, I see that it is decorated in much the same way as the foyer. Yellow walls and gold furnishings. There is a double bed against the back wall, a table and chairs by a window to the left, a television hangs on the wall opposite the bed and there is a wardrobe and dressing table to the right. A cabinet, just along from the dressing table, houses a kettle and any necessary accompaniments to make tea or coffee. Melody walks over to a door, which is to the left of the bed.

"This is the ensuite," Melody says as she switches on a light and I peer around the door. The bath tub is larger than I thought it would be, and the whole room sparkles where it has been cleaned.

"This is perfect," I say as I proceed to tell Melody that I will take the room for the night.

"Wonderful dear. It's sixty pounds for the night, and breakfast is served in the dining room between eight and ten. There is also a communal room, if you feel that you would like to relax in the company of others." She smiles at me and I find it no effort to smile back, her kind nature making me momentarily forget my troubles. "If you could just follow me back downstairs, then we can get you signed in."

"Great." I follow Melody back to the foyer, and she asks me to sign the guest book.

"Will it just be the one night that you will be staying dear?" she asks me.

"Oh, um, I'm not really sure yet." I can barely think about what I am going to do in the next hour, let alone think about how long I want to stay here for.

"Not to worry," Melody says. "Are you here on a business trip?"

"Uh, not exactly." I don't really know how to answer the question. I can hardly say that my boyfriend mistook abortion leaflets to be mine so he went and pulled some tart to make me jealous. "I just need a bit of a time out."

"Ah, career girl huh?" I just smile at her and she seems to take my smile as a yes. "Well, I don't have anyone booked into this room for a few days, so you are welcome to stay until then."

"Thank you," I say, grateful that she doesn't ask any more questions about why I am here. Melody hands me the key to my room and then shows me around the dining area and the communal room. The dining room has six oak tables, with matching oak chairs and the yellow theme continues in here. White tablecloths are edged in pretty lace, and deep red curtains hang at the windows. The communal room blows me away. In the middle of the back wall is the most intricate fireplace that I have ever seen. It is beautiful and is definitely the main feature of the room. There are comfortable armchairs situated around the fireplace, and then over by the window are two tables and beautifully upholstered chairs. There isn't anyone in here at present, but I imagine that the guests are attracted to the warmth and comfort of this room. I can just picture myself curling up in one of the chairs, fire roaring, reading a good book and sipping a glass of wine.

"Well, that's the tour over," Melody says, diverting my attention back to her.

"This really is a beautiful place Melody."

"Thank you dear. I hope that you enjoy your stay here, however long that may be." She smiles at me and I thank her again before going to retrieve my holdall from the car. When I return, Melody is in the foyer and I open my handbag, pulling out my purse. Luckily, I have some cash on me, so I pull out sixty pounds for tonight and hand it over to her. "You know that you don't need to pay until you have finished your stay," she says, clearly taken aback at me having the money ready to give her.

"Oh," I say, not at all accustomed with the way Melody does things. Usually, in a hotel, you pay up front before they allow you to set foot in the room. I feel a little bit silly that I practically thrust the money in her face.

"It's okay dear, I know that other places require money upfront, but I have never had any problems in asking guests to settle their bill." She really does seem like such a lovely, trusting lady. I pull my hand back from her and shove the money back into my purse. I smile shyly and make my way up the stairs, holdall in hand. I reach my room and unlock the door, closing and locking it behind me. I leave my holdall by the door and walk over to the bed. I sit on the edge and pull my phone out of my pocket. I find Lydia's name and give her a call. She answers on the first ring.

"Stacey," Lydia practically shouts down the phone. "Where the bloody hell are you? I thought that you were coming to mine?" I can hear the panic in her voice, and I feel bad that I didn't call her back earlier.

"Sorry Lyd, I didn't mean to worry you. I just, I couldn't come to yours."

"Why not?"

"Because, your flat is the first place that Jake would think to look for me." Lydia stays silent and I know that Jake has already been round there, but I ask the question anyway. "He came round, didn't he?"

"Yes." Lydia's voice is quiet.

"See, I knew that he would."

"I know that you don't want to hear this right now, but, he was a mess Stace." She sounds like she feels sorry for him.

"He's drunk," I reply, bluntly.

"No babes, he wasn't drunk. I think that maybe the shock of everything has sobered him up somewhat. Paul is still with him. He has gone back to yours, with Jake, so that he can keep an eye on him." Although I am mad with Jake, my heart aches at the thought of him hurting. His actions may be beyond repair, but it doesn't mean that I can turn my love for him off. I can't just stop caring about him. I wish that I could.

"Lyd, I need to ask you to do me a favour."

"Okay. What is it?"

"I know that this is terrible timing, but, could you run The Den for me? I can't face being there right now. I know that it is a lot to ask, but I can't risk seeing Jake until I am ready. If he knows that I am at The Den, then he will show up."

"Consider it done," Lydia replies, no hesitation in her answer.

"Thanks Lyd."

"So, are you going to tell me where you are?" she asks.

"I'm just at some bed and breakfast. I saw it as I was driving, and I just stopped and asked if they had any rooms." I shrug my shoulders, even though I know that Lydia can't see me.

"How long will you be there for?"

"I don't know. I just need some time to process everything." I sigh in frustration at how things have dramatically changed in the last couple of hours. "So, are you going to tell me properly how things went with Paul now?" I ask, changing the subject.

"He was great Stace. I told him everything, including how I took drugs. He said that he likes me too much to walk away." She sounds giddy with happiness.

"That's awesome Lyd. I'm so happy for you." Even if my own love life is in tatters, at least Lydia's is improving.

"Thanks babes."

"Listen Lyd, I think I'm going to try and get some rest now. I feel exhausted all of a sudden."

"Okay. Call me tomorrow, yeah?"

"Sure. Love ya."

"Love you too babes."

"Bye." I hang up the phone and it immediately starts to ring. Jake's name flashes across the screen and I chuck the phone on the bed as if it has burned me. I can't speak to him yet. I lie down and curl up into a ball. The tears start to fall again and the pain slicing through my heart is horrendous. After everything Jake and I have been through, why the hell did it have to come to this?

<u>Chapter Fourteen.</u>

<u>Stacey.</u>

I must have fallen asleep because when I open my eyes, the room is pitch black. I sit up, feeling disorientated, and I feel my way across the bed to the bedside lamp. I switch it on and rub my eyes, which are sore from crying. I make my way over to the window and close the curtains before going into the ensuite. I use the facilities and then stare at my reflection in the mirror. My eyes are puffy and red-rimmed. My face is pale, and my eyes convey all of the misery that I am feeling. I splash my face with water and then dry myself on the plush yellow towel that is hanging on the heated rail. I return to the bed and climb under the duvet, failing to take off my clothes. I don't have the energy to get undressed. I pick up my phone, which is still on the bed from earlier. I have five more missed calls, one text message and a voicemail, all from Jake. My stomach churns as I contemplate deleting the text and the voicemail without reading or listening to them. It takes me a few minutes to decide that I can't delete them. As much as I know that it would be best to ignore them, I have to look. Curiosity gets the better of me and I open the text message.

Stace, please speak to me. I'm such an idiot. Not being able to speak to you is killing me. I'm so sorry for what I did. Please, just think about calling me back. I love you

more than you will ever know, Jake x x x

My breath catches as I re-read the message a few times. *Why did he not just ask me about the damn leaflets? Why did he have to go and chat up some other woman? I could be at home with him right now if he hadn't jumped to conclusions.* I take a deep breath and, before I can chicken out, I listen to my voicemail. I put it on loud speaker and wait for the message to begin.

'Baby, I am so sorry. I know that I have said that already,

but I need you to believe how sorry I am. I wasn't thinking

straight after finding those abortion leaflets. I just....... I

thought the worst, and I shouldn't have done that. I know that

you would never do that to me.'

I hear his voice break at this point, and it makes my heart constrict with pain.

'I don't want to lose you Stace. We have come through so

much. I don't want us to be over. I didn't mean to hurt you.

I love you so much. I don't know how to be without you.

You are my whole fucking world. I wish I could take it back.

Please talk to me. Please.......'

The message ends with the sound of Jake breaking down and then cuts off. I delete it straight away. I can't listen to that again. The pain in his words and the anguish in his voice makes me want to get in my car and go to him. It would be so easy, but I know that I would regret it. I need to give myself time to decide what I want to do. I turn my phone off and place it on the bedside table. I lie there, staring at the ceiling, for god knows how long before I decide to turn the television on. I just need some sort of background noise to try to distract me. I need to stop hurting, just for a little while. I flick through the channels, but seeing as it is just after three in the morning, there is nothing decent on. I mindlessly stare at the screen whilst some woman gives the weather report. I don't take in anything she is saying. I just stare and will myself to feel numb. My head whirrs with what I should do, and I keep replaying the events that transpired with Jake. *Can I really be with a man who would use another woman to try and piss me off? How many more hurdles am I going to have to face by staying with him? Can I really give him up? Can I throw away everything we have worked for over a misunderstanding?* My thoughts consume me until I am so tired, that I finally drift off to sleep again.

Chapter Fifteen.

Stacey.

I don't wake up in time for breakfast, which is just as well seeing as I have no appetite. It is just after eleven in the morning when I wake up. At least I managed another few hours of sleep. I still feel exhausted though. I get out of the bed and use the ensuite. I decide that running a nice, hot bath might help to relieve some of the tension in my body. I start running the water and then I go to the bedside table and turn my phone on. Before I can do anything, my phone starts to ring. It's Jake again. I toy with the idea of answering, my finger hovering over the answer button, when the ringing cuts out. I place the phone down on the bedside table and return to the ensuite. I wait for the bath to fill up, shutting the door. I take my clothes off, feeling icky that I slept in them all night. I finish running the bath and then get in, enjoying how the hot water makes my skin tingle.

I stay in the bath until the water becomes luke warm. As I drag my weary body out, I dry myself and I hear my phone buzzing in the next room. I ignore it for the time being, taking my time to get dry. I then go to my holdall and take out a pair of leggings and my off the shoulder jumper. Or my comfy jumper as I call it. I grab some clean underwear and then go back to the ensuite to get dressed. I dry my hair with the towel and tidy up the ensuite, ensuring that I have dried any water on the floor. My phone starts to buzz again and I sigh as I roll my eyes and walk over to it. Jake's name appears across the screen again and I wait for the call to end. I desperately want to speak to him, but I still need time. I decide to call Lydia.

"Hi babes," she says as she answers the phone. "How are you feeling today?"

"I'm okay," I reply, sullenly.

"Really?"

"No."

"Look Stace, I know that this is a shitty situation, but, maybe it would help to talk to Jake?" I know that she means well, but with her saying that I should speak to him, it is slowly chipping away at any resolve I have to ignore his calls.

"No," I reply, bluntly as determination courses through me to stand my ground. I hear Lydia sigh and I know that she is frustrated with my stubbornness.

"Jake has been round here again this morning." I groan out loud at her words. He can't hound my best friend. No wonder she wants me to speak to him.

"Was he hoping that I would be there this time?"

"I think so. I had to tell him that you have gone away for a few days. He looked devastated Stace. Paul said that Jake was pacing the house all night long, trying to figure out where you could have gone."

"I'm sorry that he is bothering you Lyd."

"Don't you apologise. This is all my fault anyway."

"Oh no, don't you dare........" I don't get to finish my sentence as Lydia cuts me off.

"Stacey Marie Paris, I know what you are going to say, and I also know that this whole situation *is* my fault. I don't need you trying to tell me that it isn't. If you hadn't taken those abortion leaflets for me, then none of this would have happened. You know that as well as I do." She pauses and I hear her take in a deep breath. "Babes, I know that you are hurting, but can't you just give him a call? I know that what he did was out of order, and I'm not sticking up for him, but, you guys are made for each other."

"I will speak to him when I am ready, and that's not yet."

"Okay," Lydia replies, exasperated. "I just don't want you to regret not talking to him." I know that she means well, but I need to get off of the phone.

"I need to go Lyd, but I will call you tomorrow."

"Oh, okay." She sounds a little shocked that I am ending the call, but I don't need to hear her fighting Jake's corner any longer.

"Speak to you soon."

"Bye Stace." I hang up the phone and let out a groan of frustration. I think about what Lydia said, and I scroll through the phone and find Jake's name. I stare at his name and am so close to pressing the dial button, but I can't make myself do it. I throw the phone down on the bed and decide that I need to get out of this room. I need to go for a walk. I put my shoes on, grab my handbag and exit my room. I leave my phone on the bed. I don't want to take it with me. I leave the bed and breakfast and there is no sign of any other guests. I walk through the car park and head left, along the main road. I don't worry about being seen by Jake as he has no idea where to look for me. I walk about ten minutes along the road and I come across a newsagents. I decide to take a look inside and maybe pick up a newspaper. I enter the shop, which is actually bigger than it appears from the outside, and I take a look around. I grab a daily newspaper to read, just for something to do. As I look around the store, I notice a stationary section near the back. I peruse the notepads and pens and decide that a spot of writing may take my mind off of my personal life. I pick up a couple of notepads and a pack of pens and take them to the counter to pay. After paying and leaving the shop, I head back to the bed and breakfast. Walking along, I am scared to death when a car starts beeping its horn at me. I jump in shock and freeze on the spot, my thoughts immediately thinking that it is Jake. As I look up though, I see that it is Martin's car. He pulls over, puts his hazard lights on, and jumps out of the driver's seat.

"Baby girl!" he screeches at me as he comes running around the car. "What are you doing here?" he asks as he envelopes me in a hug. I take comfort in his arms holding me as I feel fresh tears spring to my eyes. *No Stacey, don't fucking cry now!* When I don't answer, Martin steps back and takes a proper look at me. "Baby girl, what's wrong?" he asks, concern replacing his happy demeanour from a few seconds ago. Instead of answering him, I let the tears fall. I can't hold them back any longer. Martin puts his arm around my shoulders and guides me towards his car. He opens the passenger door and manoeuvres me into the passenger seat. The sobs rack my body as he puts my seatbelt on and then hurries around to the driver's side. Martin starts to drive, and I don't ask where we are going. I don't care where we are going either. I let all the emotions flow through me as I continue to let the pain take over. Anger, hurt, betrayal, disappointment, and sadness consume me. I felt like my heart was shattering into a million pieces last night, but right now, in this moment, I know that I am heartbroken and I worry that it may never be repaired.

Chapter Sixteen.

Stacey.

I return to the bed and breakfast just after six, after spending the remainder of the afternoon with Martin at his house. I promised that I would call him tomorrow before I waved him off, assuring him that I would be okay. He offered for me to stay at his, but I didn't think that it was fair of me to put him out like that. I also didn't want to annoy Melody by not letting her know if I was staying again or not. I enter the foyer and Melody comes waltzing out of the communal room.

"Hello there dear," she says, smiling at me.

"Hi Melody. I just wanted to make sure that it was okay for me to stay again tonight?"

"Of course it is. You look a little pale dear, are you feeling okay?" she asks me, her brows furrowing with concern.

"It's just been a long day." I don't care to divulge my personal problems to her. I spent the afternoon doing that with Martin and I feel drained. "If you're not too busy, could I possibly have a large glass of white wine?" I ask her, feeling that I need something to drink after an emotional day.

"Coming right up. You go on through to the communal room and I will bring it in to you."

"Thank you," I say as she rushes off into the dining area. I enter the communal room and choose to sit in one of the chairs by the window. I place my handbag and my bag of shopping, that I got from the newsagents earlier, on the table. I am the only person in here and it feels peaceful. I stare out of the window and enjoy the view of the gorgeous sunset. Melody comes in a few moments later with my glass of wine. She places it on the table in front of me.

"There we are dear. I will add it to the tab for your room."

"That's great," I say, hoping that I won't have to force myself to make polite conversation.

"I'm so glad that you have decided to stay another night. It's nice to have someone young here. Don't get me wrong, I love anyone coming here, but most of the people who walk through that door are old fuddy duddies." She chuckles and I laugh along with her. It's the first time I have laughed in two days, and it feels good. "Anyway, I must dash, lots of work left to do before tomorrow." She gives me a wink and then leaves the room. I shake my head and smile. She really is a character, and her easy nature has made me feel so comfortable here. I pick up my glass of wine and take a sip. I close my eyes as the cool liquid slides down my throat. I take another sip and let my mind drift to the conversation that Martin and I were having earlier. Martin was wonderful. He let me vent, cry, and then vent some more. He listened to my fears and worries. He didn't try to convince me to speak to Jake. He was just there for me, and that is just what I needed. I take another sip of wine and nearly drop the glass when someone clears their throat right behind me. I turn around to see who it is and am gobsmacked by the person standing there.

"I'm sorry, I didn't mean to make you jump." *Holy shit, it's Doctor Bradley.* He smiles at me and my mouth drops open in surprise. He indicates to the chair on the other side of the table. "Do you mind if I join you?"

"Uh, no, not at all." *Why would he want to sit with me?*

"It's Stacey, right?" he asks as his eyes linger intently on my face.

"Yeah." I don't know what else to say. I sit, awkwardly, racking my brains for something to say. He has a glass of scotch in his hand, and he takes a sip.

"So, how are you?" he asks, placing the scotch glass on the table.

"Uh, I'm okay thanks. You?"

"I'm great. How's your friend? Lydia, isn't it?" *Should Lydia's doctor be asking me this?*

"Oh, she's fine." I feel my face frown. "Excuse me for being blunt but, can I ask why you wanted to sit with me?" I decide that I don't have the energy or the inclination to pussy foot around someone right now.

"Oh, well, I just moved back to the area and I don't really know anyone. I saw you sitting here and recognised you from the other day. I can leave though if you like?" He looks a little wary and I instantly feel like a bitch for being so blunt.

"No, it's fine. I'm sorry. I'm just not very good company at the moment. I didn't mean to come across as rude." The guy is only looking for some friendly chit chat. I bet he wishes that he hadn't bothered coming over now.

"No worries. So, you don't mind if I sit with you then?" his striking eyes look to me for confirmation.

"No, of course not." I smile at him. "So, how long have you been staying here?" I ask him, feeling that I now need to make a little bit of effort to show that I am not just some rude bitch.

"A couple of weeks now. I just moved back from America."

"Wow. Why would you do that? I would love to live out there." It has always been a dream of mine to go to America. One day I hope that I will make that dream come true. Doctor Bradley chuckles at my reaction.

"I guess you could say that I felt homesick. I missed certain aspects of living here. I also have a brother who I am hoping that I can reconnect with. I left on bad terms with him, and I am hoping to gain back his trust." He looks sad as he speaks. I can't help but feel sorry for him.

"Oh." Well, that conversation turned a little more serious than I thought that it would. I'm a little surprised that he has just divulged personal information to me, seeing as I am a virtual stranger to him. "I'm sorry to hear that." There really is nothing else that I can say at this point.

"It's my own fault. I acted like a complete ass when I was younger." He stares out of the window as he speaks. "I am hoping to change my brother's opinion of me, and I'm hoping that he will be able to see that I am not the same person that I once was." His head turns and his eyes lock with mine.

"I'm sure that it will all work out."

"Fingers crossed." He smiles and clears his throat. "So, what brings you to this bed and breakfast?"

"Um, let's just say that I needed a time out from life." I give him the same reason that I gave Melody.

"Huh. I'm guessing that there could be a man involved in that statement." I let a sad smile form on my lips, not bothering to hide the fact that he has hit the nail on the head.

"I would rather not talk about it." I'm not about to place my trust in this guy. He may be a doctor, but that doesn't mean that I have to tell him my secrets. I take a few gulps of my wine and Doctor Bradley nods towards my glass.

"Another?" he asks, picking his scotch glass up off of the table.

"No thanks. I really should be getting back to my room." I stand up and the doctor does the same. He holds his hand out for me to shake. I place my hand in his and I don't fail to notice how he tightens his grip on me.

"It was nice talking to you Stacey. We should do it again soon." He flashes me a killer smile and I quickly pull my hand away, feeling like I am betraying Jake by being near this guy. I can appreciate that he is handsome, but that's as far as it goes. I don't get butterflies from looking at him. I don't feel a blush creeping over my cheeks. I don't feel my sex stir with need at the thought of his skin on mine. Jake has officially ruined me for any other man. I doubt that anyone will ever make me feel the way that Jake does. I smile at Doctor Bradley before picking up my bags off of the table. I turn and exit the communal room, making my way up the stairs to my room. I unlock the door and enter my room, putting my bags on the floor and locking the door behind me. I feel my body sag against the closed door and I close my eyes, hoping to god that I can find a way out of the hell that I am feeling sometime soon.

Chapter Seventeen.

Stacey.

It's six in the evening, and I have spent the whole day locked in my room, writing. I woke up this morning and took out the notepads and pens, that I bought from the newsagents yesterday, and I sat by the window, pouring my heart out onto the pages in front of me. It feels therapeutic to write about the way that I am feeling. It also lets me maintain a sense of privacy that I have put all of my emotions into characters that I have made up. I have been running on caffeine all day long. I didn't make it to breakfast again this morning, but I still have no appetite. I know that I should really eat, but I have been so consumed with getting my thoughts down on paper that I haven't thought about anything else. My phone has been off all day. It's been quite nice to shut myself off from the outside world. I know that I need to switch it on and check in with Lydia and Martin, but I am enjoying my last few moments of peace before I do that. I sip the last of my coffee and walk over to the bedside table. Picking up my phone, I turn it on and wait to see what messages await me today. I have two messages, one from Lydia and one from Martin. They are both just asking how I am doing. I have nothing from Jake. I feel a pang of disappointment within me. I know that I asked for space, and I know that I am the one who has been ignoring his calls, but I would hate to think that he has given up on me. My mind is still all over the place as I realise how ridiculous that sounds. I want him to leave me alone, but then I'm disheartened that he hasn't called. I need to get my shit together. I decide to give Martin a call to distract my confused thoughts.

"Baby girl!" Martin exclaims as he answers the phone. "How are you doing?" His voice softens as he asks me the question.

"I'm okay Mart. How are you?"

"Oh, I'm just peachy." I sense a hint of sarcasm in his answer.

"What's wrong?" I ask, feeling concern for my friend.

"I don't know if I should tell you."

"Why not?"

"Because it's work related." I instantly know that his problem is with Jake and I sigh into the phone. I don't want him to feel like he can't talk to me just because Jake is his boss.

"You can tell me you know. I'm not going to fall apart at the mention of his name." I would have done two days ago, but I feel like I can't cry over Jake any more than I already have.

"Well, to put it bluntly, Jake has been a fucking nightmare. He was in work today, and all he did was shout and ball at anyone who spoke to him. Honestly, it was horrendous. He's clearly not handling this situation very well."

"I'm sorry Mart."

"What the hell are you sorry for? You haven't done anything wrong." He sounds genuinely perplexed by my apology.

"Well, the reason he is in a foul mood is because of me. I'm just sorry that he is taking it out on everyone else."

"Don't. Don't you dare apologise for his behaviour. He only has himself to blame baby girl." I know that Martin is trying to make me feel better, but I don't like the thought of him getting shit at work. "Listen, I know that you need your space and I totally understand that, but, can I just say something that has been on my mind since yesterday?"

"Sure." I know that I am not going to want to hear this by the tone of his voice, but I feel that I should listen to him. He has been good to me, and I don't want to make him feel like his advice or opinion doesn't matter to me.

"I know that what he did to you was totally out of order. I understand that you are hurt and feel betrayed by his actions. I would be mega pissed if my partner did that to me, so please don't think that I am sticking up for him." Martin stops talking and I can practically hear his thoughts through the phone. "I keep running over what happened between you guys in my head, and I just can't believe that Jake would have done anything with that woman. He isn't the type to cheat Stace. He shouldn't have jumped to conclusions about those leaflets, but I just keep thinking what I would have done in his shoes. I mean, if it had been me that had found those leaflets, I think I would have jumped to the same conclusion as he did. I know that might make me a shitty person for saying that, but hurt and anger can make you do stupid things." I let out the breath that I have been holding at hearing Martin's opinion. The line stays silent as I process his words. *Have I blown this out of proportion? Should I give Jake the benefit of the doubt?*

"Stace?" Martins voice interrupts the questions swirling around my head.

"Yeah."

"I thought that you had put the phone down for a minute." Martin sounds a little wary.

"No, I'm still here."

"I'm sorry baby girl, I know that you probably didn't want to hear what I just said, but I just thought that maybe it might help you decide what to do."

"It's certainly given me something to think about." I'm not pissed off with Martin for voicing his opinion. He's just trying to help, but I know that whatever I decide to do, he will support me. As will Lydia.

"Do you feel like you might return to the real world soon?"

"Maybe. I don't know. Listen Mart, I'm going to go and grab a drink and then have an early night."

"Okay baby girl. Make sure that you don't stay away too long."

"I won't." I smile as we say our good byes and I hang up the phone. I scroll to the pictures on my phone, looking at the ones of Jake and I together. We look so happy in each and every one. *Am I really prepared to throw away what we have? Can I get past the hurt that he has caused me? Can I repair my broken heart?* I sit there and replay my conversation with Martin over and over in my head, willing myself to look at it from Jake's point of view. I can sort of see what Martin was saying. I understand that as a human being, we can sometimes over react and judge things without knowing the facts. I get that. I think that, what I am struggling with, is that fact that Jake allowed another woman to touch him. I don't know if I can get over that. A message pings on my phone and I see that it is from Jake. I take a deep breath and open the message.

Chris Brown, 'With You.'

I love you. Jake x x x

I close the message and search for the song that he has referred to. I have it on my music playlist. I start to play the song and I listen to the words. The words are clearly relevant to how Jake feels. It gets to a certain line in the song and I am shattered. When the words 'cause if you ever let me go I would die' are sung, it penetrates straight to my heart. By the time the song finishes, I am a mess. The tears that I thought I had cried enough of have re-emerged. I make my way over to the bed and torture myself by listening to the song on repeat, the thought of getting a drink disappearing from my head. It's like I need to punish myself in some way by listening to the lyrics. I am the reason that Jake is struggling and I hate the thought of it. I eventually drift off to sleep, the music playing in my subconscious, making my dreams just as painful as my reality.

Chapter Eighteen.

Stacey.

I am up and dressed in time for breakfast this morning. I figured that after two days of eating nothing, I really could do with some food inside me. I make my way down to the dining room just before nine o clock to be greeted by Melody as soon as I enter the dining room.

"Morning dear," she says to me in her usual cheerful manner. "Come and take a seat." She guides me to a small table by the window and I thank her as I sit down. "You're the first person to show up for breakfast this morning."

"Really?"

"Uh huh. They must all be having a lie in. Well, what can I get for you dear? Full English? You could do with some meat on those bones of yours." I take no offence to her comment. I don't think it is in her nature to be malicious in any way what so ever.

"A full English sounds great. Thanks Melody."

"Excellent." Melody potters through a door to the back of the dining room, which I presume is the kitchen. I spot a table with drinks on it near the back of the room. I walk over to it and pour myself a glass of orange juice as well as a cup of coffee. I take the drinks back to my table and sit down, enjoying the aroma of the coffee beans. As I take my first sip, I see Doctor Bradley walk into the dining room. He looks very smart in black suit trousers and a crisp, white, long sleeved shirt.

"Good morning," he says as he acknowledges me.

"Morning." He gives me a megawatt smile and then makes his way over to the table with the drinks on. Melody returns to the room, carrying my breakfast.

"There we are dear. Enjoy," she says as she puts the plate in front of me. My eyes boggle at the amount of food on the plate. The breakfast is huge. I quickly mask my shock at all of the food and proceed to thank Melody. She gives me a smile and then turns to Doctor Bradley. "Good morning Doctor. What can I get for you this morning?" she asks him.

"Whatever she's having," he says as he nods to my plate.

"Fabulous. Take a seat and I'll be back in a jiff." She once again leaves through the door to the back of the room. Doctor Bradley chooses to sit at the table opposite me. I pick up a piece of toast and take a bite. My stomach growls in response. I can feel Doctor Bradley's eyes on me as I chew my piece of toast. I look up at him and he quickly looks away, obviously trying to hide the fact that he was watching me. I decide that I don't particularly want him gawping at me eating my breakfast, so I make a snap decision.

"Would you like to join me?" I ask, gesturing to the vacant chair opposite me. If he sits with me, then maybe he will feel the need to stop staring.

"And there was me thinking that you would never ask." He gets up, chuckling to himself, and brings his drink with him. Melody returns to the dining room with his breakfast and places it on the table as he sits down.

"This is just what I need to start the day," he says, eyeing the food appreciatively. Melody chuckles and I can see her eyes darting from Doctor Bradley and over to me. I squirm slightly in my seat. I can practically see the excitement in her eyes that we are sitting together.

"You two would make a cute couple," she says before she notices another guest walk into the dining room. She chuckles again as she walks away and I decide to ignore her comment. I have no interest in Doctor Bradley in that way.

"So," I start to say, not wanting Doctor Bradley to think too much about Melody's comment. "Busy day at the surgery Doc?" I ask him as I place a piece of bacon in my mouth.

"Actually, I'm only in the surgery this morning. I have the afternoon off, and I intend to visit my brother and try to talk to him."

"Oh. Well, good luck. Not that you will need it. I am sure that he will be able to see that you have changed, whoever he may be," I say, trying to be positive.

"Thanks. I think that I might need more than luck though." I can see on his face that he is worried about how this meeting with his brother might go.

"Hey, you will be fine. Family is important. I'm sure that the two of you will work out your differences." I give him a reassuring smile and he returns it, his face relaxing.

"I hope so." He takes a bite of his sausage and swallows before speaking again. "Have you got any plans today?"

"I thought that I would do some writing."

"Writing?" Doctor Bradley asks. It is at this point that I realise that he won't have a clue that I love to write. I wasn't exactly very forthcoming with information the other night.

"It's my dream to become a published author. So, whilst I am here, having a time out, it seems like a perfect opportunity to get some writing done."

"Wow. That's awesome. What kind of stuff do you write?" he asks, seeming genuinely interested.

"Well, my first novel is a crime novel, but I didn't bring my laptop with me so I can't do anymore to that at the moment. I did start working on a new novel yesterday, which is about romance and heartbreak." I don't tell him that it is due to my current love life that I have decided to put pen to paper. I wouldn't want anyone to read it and compare it to the life that Jake and I shared up until a couple of days ago.

"Well that's informative," Brad says sarcastically but playfully.

"Hey," I say as I smack his arm gently. "If I tell you anymore details then you won't buy the book when I'm rich and famous," I tease back. It feels good to have some friendly banter.

"Well, I would expect a free copy of course." He laughs and I laugh along with him. I put my knife and fork down and finish drinking my coffee. I feel bad that I have left half a plateful of food, but I couldn't eat another bite. I am absolutely stuffed. Doctor Bradley mops his plate up with his last piece of toast and then sits back, his eyes moving to my plate.

"Weak effort Stacey," he says, shaking his head at me. "What's wrong with this bacon?" he asks as he points to a couple of rashers left on my plate.

"I'm too full to eat anymore." Doctor Bradley takes this as a cue to take a rasher off of my plate and eat it. My mouth falls open. "Did you really just take food off of my plate?" I ask, astonished.

"I did."

"But, you're a doctor."

"So?"

"But, you hardly know me. How do you know that I haven't got some sort of illness or something?" Surely as a doctor, he must be a little more cautious about germs.

"I'm not worried about eating anything that you have touched. Besides, I would like to think that we have some sort of friendship going on here, and friends eat each other's bacon." His eyes twinkle as his gaze moves to my lips. I feel a little awkward at him looking at me in this way. I fidget in my seat and put my coffee cup down on the table, just for something to do. "Anyway, I best be going. Patients to see and brothers to visit," he says as he stands up, thankfully leaving me no room to comment on his words about us forming a friendship.

"I hope it goes well for you."

"Me too. Fancy grabbing a drink later? It will either be in celebration, or I will be trying to drown my sorrows."

"Sure." I smile at him as he leaves the dining room, wondering if I have made the right decision to join him for a drink later.

Jake.

"Is this really the best that you can come up with?" I shout at Martin. He sits on the other side of my desk looking petrified.

"I'm..... I'm sorry sir, but I think that it is a great idea for the Waters Industries summer ball." His voice is timid, which is hardly surprising seeing as I am acting like a complete and utter asshole towards him. I know that he doesn't deserve to face my wrath, having done nothing wrong, but I can't help it. I am fucking miserable and I am making that known to everyone around me.

"No. It's not good enough. Go away and think of something else." I wave him away with a flick of my hand. Martin doesn't need telling twice, and he quickly gathers up the paperwork that he brought in with him and leaves my office. I hang my head and feel ashamed of myself. I am not the type of person to belittle my employees like that. I hate what I have turned into in the last few days, but I can't seem to control the emotions flowing through my body. I shouldn't even be at work. My head is not here. My head, and my heart, are with Stacey. I hate myself for what I have done to her. I hate that I have hurt her. And I hate that I didn't have enough faith in her to just ask her about the fucking leaflets in the first place. I sigh and pick up my mobile phone. I haven't tried to contact her since yesterday. I wonder if she read my message. I wonder if she listened to the song that conveys how my heart feels right now. I'm trying to give her the space that she needs, but it is so fucking hard. I just wish that she would speak to me. I scroll to her name in my phonebook and am about to try and call her, when my office door flies open. I look up, in the hope that it might be her, only to be disappointed that it is Brad.

"Oh for fuck sake," I say out loud. "Can this day get any worse?"

"Oh, thanks bro. That's quite a welcome that you have going on there." Brad strides in, shutting the office door behind him. He makes his way to the chair that Martin vacated minutes ago. "What's bit you in the ass today?" he asks, looking far too fucking happy for my liking.

"I've just had a shit day so far." I keep my answer short and sweet. I don't want him to know anything about how I have lost the one person that means more to me than anything else.

"More like a shit week," Brad remarks. I eye him suspiciously. *How the fuck would he know?*

"What is that supposed to mean?" I ask, cautiously.

"Well, I have some info for you, but you have to promise to listen to me before you react." I think about this for a few minutes. He has to be bluffing. There is no way that he could know what has been going on with my life. I decide to entertain him by playing along with whatever he thinks he might know.

"Go on, what is it?" I tap my fingers on my desk as I wait for him to speak.

"When I was here the other day, you got a phone call from some woman. Her name's Stacey, yes?" I instantly feel my hackles rise at his words. I grit my teeth together to refrain from reacting to him. I need to see where he is going with this. I nod to confirm that the woman phoning me was indeed Stacey. For all I know, he just saw her name on my phone when she tried to call me. "I had the pleasure of meeting her the other day when she came to the surgery with her friend. Anyway, last night, I saw her again. I recognised her and asked her if I could join her for a drink."

"What?" I shout at him, my brain picturing all kinds of scenarios and each one fills me with rage. His words are like a punch to my gut.

"Calm down, I haven't finished talking yet."

"I swear, if you have touched her, I won't be able to control my actions." My voice is filled with hate. I am hanging onto any rational thoughts by a mere thread.

"Jake, for fuck sake man, chill out." He sighs in exasperation. "Just to be clear, I haven't done anything but talk to her, so there really isn't any need for you to go all caveman on my ass." He holds my gaze, and I get the feeling that he is telling me the truth.

"Continue." It's the only word that I can form right now.

"As I was saying, I asked to join her for a drink because she looked like she needed cheering up. She is staying at the same place as me. I asked her why she was there, and all she said was that she needed a time out. I then saw her at breakfast this morning....."

"At breakfast?"

"Yes Jake, at breakfast. She was eating her breakfast in the dining room and, when I walked in, she asked if I would like to join her." I feel as if each one of his words is like a stab to my heart. *He gets to have breakfast with her? It should be me, not him.*

"Excuse me for interrupting but, where exactly are you going with this? I mean, if you are just here to wind me up, then you are doing a fucking cracking job of it."

"I'm not here to wind you up Jake. I'm here to fucking help you. God knows, I owe you a favour or two." *Help me? He wants to fucking help me?* I snort in response. "She has no idea that I am your brother."

"Well I figured that much. If she knew that you were, then I am positive that she wouldn't have spoken to you at all. Not after what I have done." I let my voice fade off, already knowing that I have told him too much.

"I'm sure that whatever you have done, it isn't as bad as some of the shit that I have done." He chuckles at his words, obviously thinking that now is the perfect time to try and crack a joke. I give him a stern look and his laughter quickly dies.

"Look, I kind of appreciate what you are trying to do here, but I don't think that she will ever be able to forgive what I did." I don't look at him as I speak. Shame consumes me once again.

"Shit, what the hell did you do?" Brad asks, his eyebrows shooting up in question.

"I would rather not talk about it."

"Okay, fair enough. I just want you to know though that I am here if you ever need to talk." I can see that he is trying to make an effort, but I don't know if Brad and I can ever salvage our relationship. It has been hanging by a thread for years. "Listen, I am meeting her later for a drink. Do you want me to call you after I have seen her?" he asks. I hate the thought of him having a drink with her. I hate the thought of him talking to her. I hate the thought of him being anywhere near her, but what other choice do I have? If I tell him to fuck off, then I will remain as clueless as I have for the last couple of days.

"Yeah." Brad smiles but I don't return it. "Where is it you said that you were staying?"

"Oh no, I'm not telling you that."

"Why the fuck not?" I bite back.

"Because, you would go straight there and try to speak to her. I can see that she means a lot to you, but for the time being, I think that you need to give her the space that she needs. I may not understand what is going on, but I know that doing the opposite of what any woman asks is just going to piss them off." I clench my jaw, knowing that he is right. *Just how much more space is she going to need though?* It may have only been a couple of days, but it feels like a lifetime.

"Fine." The buzzer goes on the intercom, interrupting our conversation.

"I better get going anyway," Brad says as he stands up. I stand up and reach across the desk, grabbing his arm to get his attention. He looks at me questioningly.

"I meant it when I said don't touch her." My tone is laced with warning.

"I'm not going to bro. Jeez, I have learnt from my past mistakes. You're just going to have to trust me on this one." He shrugs out of my grasp and walks to my office door. "I'll call you later," he says as he opens the door, and then he is gone. To say I am shocked by the conversation that we just had is an understatement. Half of me is pleased that I am finally able to find out how Stacey is, but the other part of me is extremely wary of Brad's motives. I just have to hope that he is being true to his word. Trusting Brad is like swimming in a sea of sharks with no cage.

Chapter Nineteen.

Stacey.

I have spent the whole day writing again, and it feels so liberating. At least I have managed to do something productive in the last two days, instead of just wallowing in misery. I click the kettle on to make myself a drink and my phone starts to ring. I check who is calling before answering and I see that it is Martin.

"Hey Mart, how's tricks?"

"Oh baby girl, I have had the most awful day," he says sounding glum.

"Oh no, what's happened?"

"Ugh, what hasn't happened. First of all, work was totally shite, and then Clayton phoned me to say that he wasn't coming back. He doesn't see a future for us."

"Oh honey, I'm so sorry." I feel awful for him. I know that he loves Clayton, and I was rooting for them to work out their differences. "Did Clayton say why he didn't see a future for the two of you?" I ask, ignoring the work problem for now.

"He just said that he feels like we have grown apart, and that he loves me but he isn't in love with me anymore. I had a feeling that this was coming, but, actually hearing him say it hurts like hell." My heart goes out to him. I know how he is feeling right now. I know that we are both going through different circumstances, but heartbreak is gut-wrenching, no matter what shape or form it comes in.

"Oh god. Do you need me to come and give you a hug?" I feel like such a shit friend for shutting myself away in this bed and breakfast. I should be there for him.

"I appreciate the offer baby girl, but I think that I just need to be by myself for tonight. It's a lot to take in. At the moment I just feel sad, but I know that anger will kick in shortly, and I don't want anyone to witness me screaming the place down like a baby." I hear him take a deep breath on the other end of the phone. "I really thought that he was for keeps Stace." His voice breaks and I know that this break up has deeply affected him.

"Oh Martin." The line goes silent for a few minutes as I listen to my friend weep for his broken relationship. "Please let me come and see you," I say, wanting to be there for him.

"No, I can't face seeing anyone. I feel like someone has come along and ripped my heart from my chest." I have never heard Martin talk like this before, and it scares me. Martin has always been fun, bubbly and flamboyant. Yes, he has had down moments before, but he has always tried to make a joke out of things. He isn't known for taking life too seriously. I could kick Clayton's ass for doing this to him. "I just, I feel hollow."

"I know the feeling well." Too well actually.

"It's not quite the same though, is it?" Martin says, causing me to question what he means.

"How so?"

"Well, I know that you are hurting, but, at least Jake still wants you. He loves you and would do anything to get you back. Clayton doesn't want me. He isn't going to try and fight for me." Martin's words cause my heart to thump in my chest. He doesn't say it maliciously, he's just voicing his view of both situations. *He's right. Jake has done nothing but try to get me to speak to him.* All of a sudden, I feel ridiculous that I have let this situation drag on for the last few days. Here's Martin, on the end of the phone, in bits. He has lost the guy that he loves more than anything. My guy is still waiting for me. My guy hasn't ended things with me.

"I'm sorry," I whisper into the phone.

"Don't be sorry Stace, just make sure that you are staying away from Jake for the right reasons. If you still love him and want to be with him, then make it work. I don't want you to lose him and feel like I do right now." I don't know what to say in response. I let a tear fall down my cheek. I hear Martin blow his nose into a tissue. Maybe a change of topic will help?

"How about you tell me what happened at work today?"

"Ugh, where do I start?" he says, sighing in exasperation. "Basically, I came up with this fabulous idea for the Waters Industries summer ball. I have been working on it all week long, but today, when I showed Jake my ideas, he completely shot me down. It was humiliating. He's still not handling things well." Although the change of topic gives Martin something else to focus on for a few minutes, hearing that Jake is still struggling causes a pain to travel straight to my heart.

"He shouldn't be treating you badly Martin."

"He can't help it. He's hurting. I get it." His short answer halts our conversation. I decide to change topic again.

"Listen, why don't we hit the town on Saturday night? I feel like we could both do with a good night out."

"Okay." I expected a little more enthusiasm, but then I remember how numb I felt when I left Jake in The Den car park the other day.

"Great." I inject some cheer into my voice.

"Listen, I'm going to go and take a long, hot bath. Thanks for listening to me baby girl. And, keep in mind what I said. I don't want you to lose your happy ending." I smile, even though I know that Martin can't see me. I know that he is just looking out for me.

"I'll call you tomorrow. If you need me before then though, just let me know and I will be straight there."

"Will do. Love you baby girl."

"Love you too Mart." We end the call and I feel the need for a glass of wine. Martin's words have really hit home. I leave my phone in my room and I make my way down to the communal room. When I enter, I see that Doctor Bradley is sat in the same chair that he was sat in last night when we were talking. He has a bottle of beer in his hand, and I see that there is a full wine glass on the table. He looks up at me and smiles, gesturing me over to sit with him.

"There you are," he says as I take seat opposite him. "I was beginning to think that you had stood me up." He laughs at his joke and I take a sip of my wine.

"Mmmm. I need this." I say, taking a few more sips.

"Bad day?" he asks me.

"It was okay until a few moments ago. I just finished up a call with a close friend. He's having some trouble and I feel awful that there isn't anything that I can do for him."

"That sucks, but, you seem like you have your own problems that you need to sort out before you start to worry about anyone else's."

"I may have my own problems, but my friends are important to me," I say defensively.

"Whoa, I didn't mean anything by it." He holds his hands up in surrender and I instantly feel guilty for snapping at him.

"Sorry."

"It's okay. You know, I am here if you need to offload about anything." I know that he is dying to know why I am here, but I still don't want to tell him too much. It's actually been nice having a bit of company here, but I don't expect to see him after I leave. I shake my head at him, smiling. He doesn't give up easily. I place my wine glass back on the table and let my gaze wander to the window. It's raining heavily, the sound of the rain on the glass putting me at ease. I always love it when it is raining and I am sat indoors just listening to it patter on the window. The sound relaxes me.

"Stacey?" Doctor Bradley says after a few moments, making me pull my gaze away from the window to look at his face.

"Yeah?"

"There is something that I need to tell you."

"Okay." I feel my eyebrows knit together, wandering what on earth he could have to tell me that has caused him to have such a serious look on his face. He puts his beer down and leans forward, his arms resting on his knees as he looks at me. His look is intense and it is starting to make me feel slightly uncomfortable.

"I don't quite know how to tell you this, but I feel that you have a right to know." He takes a deep breath, and his words leave me feeling more confused than ever. *Oh god, please don't let him tell me that he is some kind of deranged stalker or something? I have already had to deal with one of those, and that was enough to last me a lifetime.* "Stacey, I am Jake's brother." And just like that, I feel like the wind has been knocked out of me. I can't have heard him correctly. This must be some kind of joke.

"Excuse me?" I say, finding my voice, even if it is quiet.

"I'm Jake's brother. I know that this must be a shock, but, you had a right to know." He pauses and picks his beer back up, taking a long gulp.

"What the hell are you talking about? I don't understand. Your surname is Bradley. Jake's surname is Waters."

"My surname is Waters too. Bradley is my first name. I have called myself Doctor Bradley for years. It sounds less pompous than Doctor Waters." *Is this guy for real?*

"No, no. This is a wind up, right?" I say, my hands starting to shake.

"Afraid not." He's being deadly serious.

"Oh my god." I close my eyes and feel stupid for not spotting the connection earlier. Jake's brother moved to America. Jake's brother is a doctor. Jake's brother is called Brad. How the hell did I not put two and two together in the first place?

"I saw Jake today. He knows that I have met you. I only realised who you were when I saw you calling him the other day when I was at his office......"

"Whoa, whoa, whoa. This is too much." I am way out of my depth here. It feels like the room is closing in on me. I abruptly stand up and bolt from the room. I run up the stairs to my room, and I can hear Doctor Bradley, or just Bradley as I now know him, calling my name. I unlock the door to my room quickly and slam it shut behind me. My breathing is laboured and I feel shaky. I lean against the door and process the limited information that Bradley just told me. *Bradley is Jake's brother. Did Jake send him here to keep an eye on me? What the hell is going on with my life? Will this madness never end?* I make my way over to the bed, on shaky legs, and I sit on the edge. *How did my life become so complicated? It's like a fucking soap opera.* I almost laugh at how eventful my life has become over the last couple of months. I am broken from my thoughts by a knock on the door to my room.

"Stacey, please open the door." It's Bradley. *Fuck. What the hell do I do?* "I just want a chance to explain things to you." *Do I trust what he is saying to me? I know that Jake doesn't have a very high opinion of him. They haven't been close for years. Would Jake really want me speaking to him?* My legs seem to make the decision for me. They take me to the door and I unlock it before my brain has caught up with what I am doing. I open the door and Bradley is stood there with fresh drinks in his hands. "I thought that you may need a refill after hearing what I just told you." He holds the wine glass out to me and I take it. "Please can I come in?" he asks.

"I don't think that is a good idea."

"Please, just five minutes. If after that you want me to leave, then I will." In this moment, he seems so genuine that I decide to hear him out. I step to one side, allowing him to enter my room. I close the door behind him and walk over to the table and chairs by the window. I sit down and gesture for Bradley to sit in the chair opposite me. He takes a seat and I wait to see what he has to say.

"I'm sorry if I went about telling you that Jake is my brother all wrong, but it didn't feel right to keep it from you any longer." He puts his beer down on the table and runs one of his hands through his hair. The action makes me picture Jake, seeing as it is something that he also does. I study Brad's face and, now that I know they are brothers, I can see similarities. They both have the same strong jaw line, the same shaped nose, and similar striking eyes. "When I went to see Jake today, I told him that you were staying at the same place as me."

"Oh god, does that mean that Jake knows where I am?" I ask, panic engulfing me.

"No. I refused to tell him where we were staying." I breathe a sigh of relief at his words. "I have done some awful things to Jake in the past. I have fucked up in so many ways, but he has always helped me out of the shitty situations that I found myself in. I don't know how much you know of mine and Jake's past."

"Not much. He doesn't really talk about you."

"I figured as much. If you knew half of the stuff that I had done, then you probably wouldn't even give me the time of day. When we were younger, we were close, but as we got older, I became jealous of Jake. He was always the together one. He always knew that he wanted to be a successful business man, and he made that happen. I resented his success, so I tried to piss him off in other ways. Before I left for America, Jake was seeing this girl. I was always a bit of a jack the lad, and anything Jake had, I wanted. Jake wasn't serious about the girl, but I didn't know that at the time. I slept with her behind Jake's back, and then I took her to America with me." I gasp at his admission. "It's safe to say that Jake lost all trust in me at that point. I think that it hurt him that, as his brother, I could do something like that to him. You can imagine how he first reacted when I told him that I had met you." He pauses and stares at the floor, clearly ashamed of his actions. "I haven't been in Jake's life since the day that I left, but I still know how he works. He's always been the same, but I have never seen him like this. He's a mess. He's suffering, and I think that you are suffering too. I know that I don't really know you, but I feel like we have a connection. I just want to help the both of you in any way that I can. I don't know the ins and outs of what has happened between you and Jake, but I know that he regrets whatever it is that he has done. He's a good guy Stace. Don't tell him that I said this, but he's one of the best. Don't let a mistake he made ruin what you two have together." He takes a swig of his beer and I am left reeling from his confession. He looks at his watch and sighs. "I guess my five minutes is up." He stands and starts to walk over to the door. He places his hand on the door handle and turns to look at me. "If you need to talk, I'm in room number twelve. Thanks for listening to me." With that, he opens the door and leaves my room. I sit in complete shock. I grab my wine glass and drain the whole thing in one go, slamming the glass back down on the table when I have finished. *Well, fuck me.*

<u>Jake.</u>

My phone rings and I see Brad's name across the screen. I answer immediately.

"Is Stacey okay?"

"And hello to you too."

"Cut the shit Brad." I'm not in the mood for idle chit chat right now.

"Jeez, you really need to loosen up bro." I clench my jaw in frustration.

"Just tell me how she is." It took every ounce of willpower that I possess not to follow him to wherever he is staying earlier and see how Stacey is for myself.

"Honestly, I don't know. I told her that I am your brother."

"Fuck." *Why the hell did he do that? I don't want Stacey to think that I have been keeping tabs on her by using him.*

"Yeah. To say that she was shocked is an understatement, but I guess that is hardly surprising. She ran off when I first told her and locked herself in her room, but I managed to get her to let me in to speak to her."

"Wait a fucking minute. You were in her room?" *He shouldn't be anywhere near her room.*

"Yes Jake, but I was only in there for five minutes. She listened to what I had to say, and then I left." He sounds exasperated saying this, but I don't like the thought of them being alone together, especially in the privacy of her room. I know that Stacey wouldn't do anything with him. I trust her implicitly. I just don't fucking like it. "I think that she is going to need some time to process everything that I told her. You need to leave her to think things through."

"That's easier said than done."

"I know, but you need to do this, for her sake. Keep your cool, and if anything else happens, I will phone you."

"Fine." There isn't really anything else that I can say. "I suppose I should thank you for helping me."

"Never thought I would hear you saying that to me," he chuckles.

"Me either."

"Listen, do you want to grab a beer on Saturday night? I won't pull any crazy shit, I promise."

"We'll see." I hang up the phone and chuck it beside me, on the sofa. I hope to god that Brad hasn't fucked things up further for me. I want to believe that he has changed. I want to believe that he is helping me out of the kindness of his heart, but I'm still not convinced. I guess that I will just have to wait and see what the outcome is. The trouble is, I hate fucking waiting.

Chapter Twenty.

Stacey.

I am stood on the driveway of mine and Jake's home before nine o clock in the morning. I woke up early, at the bed and breakfast, paid Melody the money that I owed for the room and any expenses, said my goodbyes, and then I left. Melody made me promise that I would pop by sometime to see her. Part of the reason that I left early was so that I wouldn't bump into Brad. After last night's revelations, I feel that is only right that I see Jake before I see or speak to anyone else. I thought long and hard about what Brad told me. It played on a loop in my mind for most of the night. I then factored in Martin's words to me over his break up with Clayton. Between the two of them, they helped me reach an answer to the soul searching that I have been doing over the last few days. I look up to the house, and I realise how much I have missed this place. It may not have been my home for long, but I feel like I belong here. There is no sign of Jake's car, so I presume that he has already left for work. I open the boot of my car and take out my holdall and handbag. I lock the car and make my way to the front door.

Jake.

I feel like shit. After drinking half a bottle of scotch last night, after talking to Brad, I am left with a pounding headache. I make my way down the stairs and to the kitchen, where I proceed to make myself a coffee, drink a pint of water, and take a couple of tablets to curb the pain in my head. I sit at the kitchen island, close my eyes and sip my coffee. After finishing the first cup, I immediately make another one. Sitting back on one of the stools, I place my head on the counter top and allow my coffee to cool. I think back to what Brad told me last night, but my thoughts are interrupted by the sound of the front door opening. I sit up and strain my ears to make sure that I'm not hearing things. When I hear the front door close a few seconds later, I quietly stand up and make my way to the kitchen doorway. If this is some fucker trying to break in, then I don't fancy their chances of getting away unscathed. As I peer around the kitchen door, I am blown away by the sight before me. I move into the hall way and just stand there, looking at the vision before me. *Stacey.* Her back is to me as she places her pink holdall on the floor and takes off her shoes. I watch her, drinking in the sight of her, almost afraid to blink in case it turns out that my mind is playing tricks on me. Her long hair is in a high ponytail, her petite frame is masked by a jumper that is slightly too big for her. She places her keys on a hook by the front door and then I hear her take in a deep breath. *She's here. She's really fucking here.* She starts to turn around and my heart feels like it is going to jump out of my chest. Her head is down as she turns in my direction, and she takes a few steps forward before she freezes on the spot. Her head whips up in surprise, and her wide eyes lock with mine. It takes every ounce of control for me to stay where I am. All I want to do is go to her, hold her, and never let her go.

Stacey.

When my eyes lock with Jake's, I freeze. He stands at the end of the hall way, his hands by his sides, his jogging bottoms hung low on his hips, and his chest bare. My heart does a flutter at the sight of him. This man takes my breath away. He may have hurt me, but that doesn't take away the chemistry that is between us. My body hums in response to him being so near. He doesn't speak. He doesn't move. He just watches me. Waiting. *It's now or never Stacey.* I came here to speak to him. I came here to repair our relationship. I came here to put the bad behind us, but as I stand here and look at him, I realise that, I don't need explanations. I don't need to rehash what happened at The Den. I don't need him to apologise over and over again. I don't need him to promise me that he won't ever hurt me again. I don't need any of those things because, deep down, I know that he loves me and I know that he would do anything for me. I know that he would never have done anything with that woman. I know that he was just looking for a reaction that day because he was hurting. I know that he regrets his actions, and I suppose that I regret mine too. We are both to blame here. If I had just been honest with him about Lydia, then none of this would have happened. I thought that I was doing the right thing by Lydia, by keeping quiet, but in the end, all I did was hurt myself and Jake. I make a promise to myself that I will never again keep anything from him, no matter who asks me to. Adrenaline pumps through my body as I start to move forwards. I take slow, steady steps towards Jake. I can see his chest rising and falling with each breath he takes. I keep my eyes locked with his as I come to a stop in front of him. I don't leave much room between us as I tilt my head to keep his eyes on mine.

"Stace........" Jake starts to speak, but I move my hand up to his lips and place my fingers over them to stop him from saying anything. I don't need him to speak. I can see everything that he wants to say just by looking into his eyes. I let my other hand come upwards and I place it on his bare chest. The heat coming from him and the feel of his skin on mine makes my body sizzle. He is the only man that has ever lit me on fire. I move my hand from his lips, and I move it to the back of his neck. His body vibrates with the need to touch me, but he is still holding back. I apply pressure to my hand behind his neck, and I bring his face down to mine. He closes his eyes as his face comes closer, and I stand on tip toes and brush my lips over his. He omits a low growl in his throat and it makes my insides turn to jelly. I close my eyes and I let my lips connect fully with his. As I move my other hand up his chest, I let it travel to my other hand and I link my hands behind his neck. I push my body into his and that is all it takes for Jake to lose control. His hands find my ass and he lifts me up. I move my legs and wrap them around his waist, still not feeling as if I am close enough to him. I open my mouth to him and our tongues entwine, our kiss deepening by the second. The desire coursing through me becomes over powering and I moan into his mouth. His hands kneed my ass and it makes my sex stir with desire. I run my hands through his hair, loving the feel of his silky locks between my fingers. I cup his face in my hands and relish in the feel of his stubble on my palms. Jake turns me and pushes me up against the wall, allowing his hands to move freely. He brings one hand up to the nape of my neck, his grip holding me firm. His other hand has snaked around my back and is holding me against him. I don't think that I will ever be able to get my fill of Jake. I whimper as he pulls his lips away from me and lets his forehead rest against mine. We're both panting, trying to catch our breath. I let my hands rest against his back, the smooth feel of his skin sending signals straight to my core.

"You came back," Jake whispers, emotion rife in his voice.

"I did." He moves his head back slightly so that he can look into my eyes.

"I fucking love you Stacey Paris." His voice cracks slightly and it makes tears sting the backs of my eyes. I don't want to cry though. I don't want to shed anymore tears. I blink a few times and I gulp down the lump that has formed in my throat.

"I know," I say, breathlessly.

"I'm so sorry that I hurt you."

"I know that too." I smile at him and he opens his mouth to speak again, but I cut him off. "Take me to bed Jake."

Chapter Twenty-One.

Stacey.

I lie in bed with Jake's arms wrapped tightly around me, my back pressed firmly to his chest and his legs entwined with mine. I lightly stroke his arm enjoying the feel of goose-bumps rising on his skin from my movements. His lips are placing soft kisses on my shoulder and the side of my neck, bringing a smile to my face. The feel of his lips on my skin makes me want to make love to him all over again. When Jake brought me upstairs, he stripped me of my clothes slowly, savouring every moment of our reconciliation. Once I was completely naked, he took his jogging bottoms off and stood before me with his arousal on display. He gently lowered me onto the bed and began to devour every inch of my body. He reigned kisses on every inch of my skin, taking his time, allowing me to become more aroused with every second that passed by. What transpired between us just now was nothing short of magical. There was nothing hurried or rushed, we simply just took our time with one another, and I loved every single moment. With my body spent, Jake pulled me into his arms and he hasn't let me go since. His strong, muscular arms make me feel secure, safe and loved. Our time apart has made me realise that I never want to be without him. He owns my mind, body and soul. He may not believe it, but my heart belongs to him. No one will ever be able to take that away from him. His teeth nip at my earlobe, sending sparks shooting down to my core. I turn my face to look at him and his lips capture mine in a slow and sensual kiss. I am still being held firmly in his arms, almost as if he is frightened to let me go. When he pulls his lips away from mine, I pout slightly, making him chuckle. His eyes hold mine. I know that I made the right choice by coming back. I know that I would have been miserable without Jake.

"What's running through that beautiful mind of yours?" he asks me, placing a kiss on the end of my nose.

"I just........ I missed you," I whisper to him.

"Oh god, I missed you too. I really thought that I had lost you." He rests his forehead against mine and closes his eyes. His words pull at my heart.

"Hey," I say softly, nudging his head with mine so that he looks at me. His eyes open and I can see that it is taking everything for him to keep control of his emotions right now. "You never lost me Jake. I will always belong to you." I pour every bit of emotion into my words. He needs to hear this. "We both made mistakes, and we are both to blame for what happened."

"No," he says abruptly, his head whipping up so fast that I am surprised that he doesn't pull a muscle. "You did nothing wrong. You were just being a good friend to Lydia. I was the one who jumped to conclusions. I was the one who got it wrong. I should have known that you would never take the life of something that was mine and yours. I know you, but when I saw those leaflets, I lost myself for a few moments, and those few moments was all it took for me to turn into a complete asshole. I will regret that day for the rest of my life." His voice fades into a whisper and I let a single tear slide down my cheek. Jake notices and kisses the tear away. His grip on me has loosened slightly, allowing me to free my hand so that I can bring it to his face. I cup his cheek in my palm, and as I look at him, I see the pain and the guilt that he is still carrying from that day. I don't want him to feel guilty. I don't want him to carry that on his shoulders. I need him to understand that we have to move past it and learn from it.

"Jake, you need to stop. I don't want you to let what happened eat away at you. If I had told you about Lydia in the first place, then none of this would have happened. I forgive what you did. I forgive all the hurt, and you need to do the same." He frowns at me as if he doesn't understand what I am saying to him. "I need you to forgive me for not telling you the truth in the first place." I can see that he wants to argue with me about how he doesn't think any of it is my fault. I give him a death stare, as if daring him to argue with me, to which he starts to smile. I feel myself relax as his gorgeous smile lights up his face.

"I love it when you look at me like that," he growls in response. Jake has always told me that there is a certain look that I do that makes him hard. And, true to form, I can feel his length pressing against my leg. He moves so that he is nestled between my legs, his body covering mine and my legs parting so that he can get comfortable. He kisses the tops of my breasts and my hands run through his hair. I sigh as his kisses start to travel downwards. My eyes close and I press my head into the pillow as he reaches my sex. He parts my legs more so that I am exposed to him.

He lightly blows over my clit and excitement races through my core. I can feel his lips hovering above me, making me wait.

"Eyes baby," he says, making me lift my head to look at him. "I want you to watch as I make you come." His words, and the glint in his eyes, make me wet with want. I watch as his tongue darts out to lick my sensitive bud. He looks up to me every so often to make sure that I am watching. It takes all of my strength not to throw my head back and cry out in pleasure. As I feel my orgasm approaching, I part my legs more, giving him more access. His fingers make their way to my opening and he inserts two, all the while keeping his lips attached to my clit. His eyes fix on mine as I start to tighten around his fingers. My hips move so that I can rub against his mouth, and I start to pant as my climax gathers speed. Jake increases the pressure slightly with his tongue, and that is all it takes to tip me over the edge. I cry out his name over and over again. My eyes are still connected with his, making my orgasm more powerful. He intently watches me as he slowly works me down from my orgasm. When I feel that I can give no more, I let my body relax onto the bed and Jake quickly climbs up my body and inserts his cock at my opening. His lips cover mine and I can taste my arousal on him. He plunges himself into me, making me scream into his mouth. I wrap my legs around his waist and push his bum with my feet, making sure that he has buried himself in me as much as possible. My hands fly up to his shoulders and I grip on for dear life as Jake starts a punishing rhythm. Straight off of the back of my first orgasm, I feel another one building. With Jake's hard thrusts, and his lips on mine, it doesn't take long for my climax to ignite. I break my lips away from his as I moan and writhe beneath his strong body. My sex pulses around his cock, and a few seconds later, Jake roars from the impact of his orgasm. As I wrap my arms around his neck, I pull his body as close to me as possible. I squeeze my muscles and bite Jake's ear lobe as he calls out my name. He collapses on top of me when he is finished and I let my hands move up and down his back. My legs are still wrapped around him, and he is still inside me.

"Fucking hell," he says quietly into my ear. I smile and place a kiss on his cheek. He places his arms by the sides of my head and lifts himself up slightly, allowing him to look at me. "That was....."

"Amazing," I finish his sentence for him.

"I'm never letting you go again." I take comfort in his words, and I know that he means them. Jake doesn't open himself up to people often, but when he does, it's pretty special. I count myself as lucky to be one of the special ones. He rolls over, taking me with him. He lies on his back, me on top of him, and I know that there is nowhere else in the world that I would rather be right now. We have been through a lot in the short time that we have known each other, but whatever we face, we always seem to come through it stronger. Every hurdle we jump brings us closer. Every obstacle that stands in our way, we manage to find a way through it. I close my eyes, and place my head on Jake's chest so that I can hear his heart beating. His heart beats for me, and mine beats for him. I will fight for this man every step of the way. Our relationship is worth every single moment of pain that we have endured. I close my eyes with a smile on my face and with the simple knowledge that I am home.

Chapter Twenty-Two.

Jake.

I am the luckiest son of a bitch in the world. I watch Stacey as she shakes her fine ass on the dancefloor. She is wearing the sexiest come fuck me heels ever, and her long legs are on display due to her wearing a pair of black, tailored shorts. The silk and lace camisole top that she wears shows off her womanly curves, and her long hair is straightened, flowing down her back, begging for me to grab hold of it and tug gently as I fuck her from behind. I have noticed several men looking at her this evening, but I stand here with a smug smile on my face, because they will never get their hands on her. She is mine. They can look all they like, but I'm the one who gets to take her home and touch every inch of her body. I am the one who makes her scream in pleasure. I am the one that she chose. Even after what I did to her, she still loves me. She still wants me, and I am going to do everything in my power not to fuck up again.

When she left me for those few days, my life went to shit. I can't function without her. I never thought that I would ever be one of those men who needs a woman in their life. I never thought that I would ever give my heart over to another person, but here I am, letting her have it. As she dances with Martin, I smile at the friendship that the two of them share. I have grown fond of Martin in the short time that I have known him, and I feel awful for the way that I have treated him at work recently. I have apologised to him for my behaviour. He was understanding and just brushed it off. Stacey told me that Martin and his partner have called time on their relationship and that she wants to support Martin as much as she can. She hasn't told me what Martin said about us, during our time apart, but I have a feeling that he was rooting for Stacey and I to work it out, and for that I will always be grateful to him. Lydia is working at The Den tonight, and I made it my mission as soon as we arrived, to apologise to her. She, like Martin, brushed the whole thing off like I had done nothing major to affect her life. Paul however is a different matter. I haven't seen, or heard from him since that fateful day. I know that he stayed with me initially, to make sure that I didn't do anything stupid, but that was the last time that I saw him. I have tried to call him, but he has been ignoring my attempts to contact him. Paul is my best friend, and one of the only people that I have trusted through my adult life, and I feel like a complete wanker for the way the news about Lydia's pregnancy was broken to him. Lydia has assured me that Paul is just busy with work, but I think that she is trying to spare my feelings. Why she would bother, I really don't know. I deserve to have them raging at me. I know that, when I do eventually see Paul, that he is going to want to have his say on the matter. I expect that, and a part of me welcomes it. I almost feel that I have gotten away with my actions far too lightly.

When Stacey walked back through the front door yesterday, she didn't want to talk about it. She didn't want to go over what happened. All she wanted to do was immerse herself in me, and I wasn't about to stop her. We spent the whole day in bed together, switching between making love and fucking like animals. It has to be one of the best days of my life. My cock stirs at the memory of her body against mine, her lips against my skin, her legs straddling me as she rode me to release. I lost count of the amount of times I made her come.

“Hey bro.” I turn to look at Brad, almost scowling at him for interrupting my thoughts. His voice next to my ear acting like a cold bucket of water being poured over my cock.

“Hey,” I say as I swig my beer. “You made it then?” I had invited Brad along tonight, seeing as he wanted us to go out for a beer anyway.

“Course I did.” He sips his drink and his attention turns to the dancefloor. I follow his gaze, and I find his eyes watching Stacey and Martin, just like I was only seconds ago. “So, you guys all good now?” he asks, nodding his head towards Stacey. I am wary of answering his questions. I still don’t trust Brad, but he did help me when Stacey was gone, so I suppose I should cut him a little slack.

“Yeah.” That’s about as much slack as I am willing to give him, but it’s more than he would have got out of me a few days ago. My attention moves to Stacey as she saunters towards me, her eyes glittering. *Jesus Christ, she is fucking stunning.* Her gaze drifts to Brad and she smiles at him to acknowledge that he is standing there. She doesn’t let her gaze linger on him for long though, returning her blue eyes to lock with mine. As she reaches me, she places her hands on my chest and lets them slide up to the back of my neck. She brings my head down and places her lips by my ear, licking my ear lobe before speaking.

"I hope that you haven't had too much to drink Mr Waters. I was hoping that we could pick up where we left off this morning." Her voice purrs in my ear and sends signals straight to my cock, who has decided to wake up again since she walked over here and pushed her tight little body up against mine. She pulls her head back and brushes her lips against mine, before pushing away from my body and turning towards Brad. "Hi Brad," she says before I can respond to the words that she whispered in my ear.

"Hey Stace," he replies, completely at ease around her. I feel a pang of jealousy that he got to know her a little whilst I was out of the picture. I push the feeling down and clench my jaw. *Relax Waters. They have barely said two words to one another. Stacey has no interest in Brad, in that way.* I try to reason with myself, but I don't fail to notice the look in Brad's eyes as he looks at her appreciatively. His gaze flicks to me and I give him a cold stare, silently challenging him to look at her like that again. He shrugs his shoulders at me and turns away as Martin comes over.

"Hi dolls," Martin says as he bumps his hip into Stacey's making her giggle. "Where are those drinks baby girl? I am fucking parched."

"I'm just about to go and get them." She turns back around to look at me and Brad. "Do either of you guys want another?" I shake my head and Brad says that he would love another beer, proceeding to down the contents of the one that he is currently holding. It is at this moment that Martin seems to realise that we have an addition to our group. He looks at Brad and I stop myself from laughing at what I imagine it about to happen. If my first proper meeting with Martin is anything to go by, then this is going to be a fucking treat. I slide my hand around Stacey's waist and bring her to my side. She looks up at me and smiles, knowing as I do, that Martin is about to unleash his personality on Brad.

"And who do we have here?" Martin asks, as he runs his eyes up and down Brad.

"Martin, this is Brad, Jake's brother," Stacey says. "Brad, this is Martin." She leaves it at that and goes silent to watch the show that Martin is about to put on.

"Hi Martin," Brad says as he holds his hand out for Martin to shake.

"Well, well, well, aren't you a treat," Martin says as he takes Brad's hand and shakes it. Brad's face changes to one of shock and I bite on my lip to stop myself from laughing. "Let me ask you something Brad," Martin says as he moves towards Brad and leans in to whisper in his ear. I can't hear what Martin has said, but from the look on Brad's face, it has clearly rendered him speechless. Brad stands there and splutters as he tries to form words, and I can no longer hold back my laughter. My body starts to shake and I can feel Stacey's doing the same.

"Uh………"

"Oh relax," Martin says, letting Brad's hand go. "God, he's just as prudish as you Jake."

"Hey, I am no prude," I say through my laughter.

"I beg to differ. There was a time when you had the same look on your face as he does right now," Martin says, smirking.

"Yeah okay." I concede defeat as he is absolutely right. I was shocked as shit when he first offered me the 'Martlove.'

"Come on baby girl," he says, taking Stacey's hand in his. "Let's go and get the drinks. Brad looks like he could do with a beer to cool down." He winks at Brad and then him and Stacey walk off, heading to the bar.

"What the fuck was that about?" Brad says, still looking shocked.

"That was the whirlwind that is Martin." I take a swig of beer, chuckling away to myself.

"Fucking hell, I don't think I have ever met someone who is so forward."

"Really?" I find that very hard to believe, knowing what some of the women were like that he used to bring home.

"Seriously bro. No woman has ever said what Martin just said to me." He sees the look on my face and then bursts out laughing himself. We stand there, roaring with laughter, and it feels good. I know that I am still wary of Brad, and I don't completely trust his intentions, but, right now, for the moment at least, it feels good to be laughing with my brother.

Stacey.

I carry mine and Brad's drink back over to where Jake and Brad stand. Martin follows behind me, carrying his cocktail. Lydia informed me that Darren has been a godsend over the last few days. It seems that my choice to hire him was a good one. She doesn't mention Stephanie, but from what I can see, she seems to be holding her own. I assure Lydia that I will return to work on Monday, which I think that she is grateful for. She has been a rock for me, running this place, but I can tell that she is tired. I feel bad that I am here having fun whilst she is working, but when I said as much to her, she just waved off my concerns and told me to enjoy myself. As I reach Brad, I hand him his drink which he thanks me for. I place my drink on the table by Jake, and am about to speak to him, when I hear Starboy by The Weeknd start to pump through the speakers. Martin's squeals behind me, grabs my hand, and drags me onto the dancefloor. Ever since the song came out, Martin has said that it is his jam. I laugh as we both shake our hips to the music, people around us making room for Martin and his flailing arms. I enjoy the beat of the music as it pumps through the system, making the dancefloor vibrate. My back is to Jake, but I can feel his eyes watching me. As the song winds down and the DJ remixes in the next song, I feel my inhibitions leave me.

Nine Inch Nails, Closer, starts to play making me very aware of Jake and his eyes roaming over my body. I turn to face him, his eyes filled with heat as I move to the beat. I feel Martin come up behind me, and I swear, he is the only guy that Jake would ever let me bump and grind with. Martin's hands hold onto my hips and I move my ass in time with his, all the while keeping my eyes on Jake. He looks like he wants to pounce on me and rip my clothes off. I turn in Martin's arms, allowing Jake a view of my ass writhing to the beat. Martin grabs my ass, making me squeal from his actions.

"Martin!" I shout at him over the music.

"Oh relax baby girl. Jake won't mind. In fact, I would say that our little dance is turning him on, if the bulge in his trousers is anything to go by." I gasp at his words.

"You shouldn't be looking at his bulge," I say, playfully.

"It's kind of hard to miss." I laugh at him and we continue to dance to the song. I feel another pair of hands on my hips from behind and Martin lets go of me, giving me a wink before he turns and starts to grind up on some unsuspecting male. I keep my body moving to the song, and I feel my hair being moved away from my neck, and lips grazing my ear.

"I wanna fuck you like an animal," Jake says along with the song, his voice low and filled with heat. My hand flies up to his neck, and I bring his lips down so they connect with my skin. As he begins a delicious assault of kisses on my neck, everything around us disappears. In my mind, it is just Jake, me and the music. His hands grip my waist tighter as I grind my ass against his crotch. I don't fail to notice the low groan that he emits. I close my eyes and enjoy the feel of him against me. As the song continues to play out, I can no longer hold onto my need for him. I move my lips to his ear so that he can hear me when I speak.

"I need you Jake, *now.*" He moves quickly, jolting me back to reality in the process. He grabs my hand, pulls me off of the dancefloor and in the direction of my office. He opens the door, and slams it shut behind us, pushing me up against the door and devouring my mouth as if he hasn't tasted me for days. I groan and claw at him, my hands roaming everywhere and it still doesn't feel like it is enough. I bite his bottom lip and our actions become frenzied. We pull at each other's clothes, our hands clumsy with our desperation for one another. I free Jake's cock and run my hand up and down it, feeling that his tip is already wet. He pushes my shorts down, sliding my thong to the side and I lift my leg and hook it around his waist. I place his cock at my opening and take in a sharp breath as Jake slams into me. I cry out, grabbing his ass, needing more friction from him. He begins a punishing rhythm as he grunts into my mouth. My back is slamming against the office door, but I don't care. All I care about right now is what this man is doing to me. Over and over again he plunges into me. My grip on his ass tightens as I barrel towards my release.

"I'm coming Jake, I'm coming," I say, breathlessly. As I feel myself freefalling through my orgasm, Jake tightens his grip on my thighs and I feel him burst inside me.

"Fuck," he shouts as I tighten my muscles around him, determined to ride both of our releases to their full potential. I place my hand over Jake's heart and I bring his hand up so that it is placed over my heart too. I want him to feel how hard it is pounding. His is pounding just as much and he stares at me, questioningly. I lick my lips and take a few deep breaths before speaking.

"It's all for you Jake," I say as I answer his silent question. "My heart beats for you, and only you." He rests his forehead against mine and, if it's possible, his heart beats even harder.

"I love you so much Stace," he whispers. "I never thought that I would be lucky enough to find the great love of my life that people talk about." He pulls his head back, and my eyes search his as he puts his feelings into words. "The very first time that I laid eyes on you, I knew that I had to have you. All those months ago, I watched you from across the dancefloor. I was mesmerized by you back then, and I still am today. I used to laugh at those blokes who gushed over their partners, but that was because I didn't understand what they had." He takes a few deep breaths before continuing. "Now I understand. You are the reason that I understand." I let my hands come up to his face, placing my palms on his cheeks. "When you agreed to go home with me that night, all those months ago, I knew that it wouldn't be the end of us. I had no idea when I was going to see you again, but I knew that it would happen. When I saw you at the Bowden Hall six months later, my heart beat so fast that I was sure that you were going to be able to hear it. You looked incredible in your red dress." He closes his eyes, obviously picturing me in the red dress. I am captivated by his words. "I can picture everything about that night as if it happened yesterday. That was the night that you stole my heart. I had no idea that I was going to fall for you so hard and so fast." Tears well up in my eyes as I swallow down the lump that has formed in my throat. Jake opens his eyes and they are glistening, just as mine are. "I promise that I will love you, cherish you and worship you until the day that I die." A tear rolls down his cheek and it breaks me. I let a sob escape my throat as this man declares his love for me. I never realised that his feelings ran just as deep as mine do for him. I press my lips to his, our tears mingling together, our breathing shallow, and our bodies heaving against one another. As our lips break apart, I wipe my thumbs across his cheeks, taking away the wetness that our tears have left. "You are my life Stacey. All I want is for you to be happy."

"I am," I say, no hesitation in my reply. He smiles and it makes my insides melt. I will never take our love for granted, and I know that we will always do everything that we can to make our relationship work. Jake places a light kiss on my nose and pulls himself out of me. I pout at the loss of him inside me, and he chuckles. Guiding me to my private bathroom, we both clean ourselves up and then make ourselves presentable to return to the main room. I go to open the office door, but Jake stops me.

"You know, if you had danced with any other man, the way that you were dancing with Martin earlier, there would have been some serious punishments in store for you lady." I raise one of my eyebrows in challenge to his words.

"Is that so?" He nods his head at me, making me want to behave badly just to see what punishments he might have in store. "Well, you could always give me a taster when we get home of what those punishments might be."

"You're a bad girl Miss Paris."

"And you love it," I say as I open the door and start to lead Jake from my office.

"More than you know." His words bring a smile to my face as we enter the main room and proceed to spend the rest of the night dancing, drinking, laughing, and having fun.

Chapter Twenty-Three.

Stacey.

Monday has been a bitch of a day, and I still have another five hours before I can finish up and go home. I have been at The Den since nine o clock this morning, catching up on everything that I have missed over the last week. Lydia came in at ten o clock to bring me up to speed with what she had done in my absence. It is now six o clock, and The Den has just opened, students filtering in already after the start of their week at college or uni. Darren and Susie are working the bar at the moment, but I am on hand for when it starts to get busy. Lydia sits at the end of the bar, waiting for me as I pour us both a drink. Non-alcoholic of course. As I finish pouring our diet coke's, I walk around the bar to Lydia and sit down beside her.

"Listen Stace, I had a thought," Lydia says, grabbing my attention. "Why don't you and Jake come round to mine for dinner on Thursday night? I think it's about time that we got Paul and Jake in the same room together and let them sort their shit out."

"I don't know Lyd." I'm wary of her idea as I know that Jake has tried to contact Paul, resulting in Paul ignoring him.

"I feel like we need to do something. I know that Paul misses Jake, he's just too stubborn to admit it."

"Is Paul really still that mad with him?" I ask.

"I don't know." Lydia shrugs her shoulders as she speaks. "I have tried to get him to talk about it, but he just shuts down. I think that he is just pissed at how the whole situation turned out."

"I know that it was bad, but if you and I can get past it, then why can't Paul?" I don't really understand why he seems to have a bigger issue with it than the rest of us.

"I think it's more to do with how Jake handled it all. Jake went from being angry, to trying to hurt you, and then he took it out on everyone around him. In all the years that Paul has known him, he said that he had never seen Jake act that way before. Paul was mad on my behalf because I was mad at how Jake had treated you." I process what Lydia is saying, but it still confuses me that Paul is having difficulty with it all.

"Let me speak to Jake first. I don't really want to walk into anything that he doesn't feel comfortable with." There is no way that I am springing this on him by just showing up at Lydia's place. We are just getting back on track and I am not doing anything to fuck up our progress. Lydia is about to reply to me when some guy goes crashing into the back of her, shoving her forward on her seat. I see her hands shoot out in front of her to stop her from smacking into the bar counter. I jump up off of my stool and whirl around to look at the guy who just knocked into her.

"HEY ASSHOLE!" I shout at him, as I move myself to stand in front of Lydia. The guy struggles to stand up straight and I see a couple of his mates laughing behind him.

"Sorry love. I tripped," he slurs.

"You tripped?" I screech at him. "Did it ever occur to you to drink less and be more fucking careful?"

"It was an accident," he says with a shrug of his shoulder.

"It may have been an accident, but your accident has resulted in you smacking into a pregnant woman." His face pales at my comment, but I am not finished with him yet. "You need to leave, now." I am filled with rage as I feel Lydia's body shaking behind me. The guy takes a step forward, obviously hoping that he is going to intimidate me.

"Who the fuck do you think you are?" he spits at me. "What's a pregnant woman doing in here anyway?" My eyes shift to look at his two pals, who are no longer laughing. They are slowly backing away instead of trying to take their repulsive friend with them. I remain where I am, hands on my hips, unwilling to let this piece of shit make me feel threatened by him.

"Get out," I say the words loud but slow just so he understands.

"I'm going nowhere sweetheart." I am about to retaliate when a voice from behind him shouts out.

"I think that you are," the voice says as the guy is pulled away from me. He stumbles backwards and falls to the floor. My eyes fly up from the sprawling mess on the floor and I see that Brad is stood there, his hands balling into fists as he leans down and says something into the guys ear. My eyes are wide as the guy scrambles to his feet and the bouncers come over to escort the guy off of the premises. I turn my attention to Lydia and put my arms around her.

"Are you okay Lyd?" I ask her, worry threatening to overpower me.

"Yeah, I'm fine. Just a bit shaken." Her voice breaks and a tear slides down her cheek.

"You need to get to the hospital and get checked over," I tell her.

"No Stace, I'm fine. I don't want to go to hospital."

"Tough."

"Stace, please, I don't want any fuss. I'm just a bit shocked that's all." She tries to plead with me, but I am taking no chances. I grab Lydia's phone out of her hand, find Paul's number, and I hit the dial button. He answers immediately.

"Hi beautiful," he says as he answers the phone.

"Uh, Paul, it's Stacey."

"Oh shit, sorry. Is everything okay?" he asks in a panic, clearly wondering why the hell I am phoning him from Lydia's phone.

"Not really. Lydia needs to get to a hospital. Some guy knocked into her so she needs to go and get checked over."

"Fuck. I will be there in five minutes." The line goes dead and I place Lydia's phone in front of her, on the bar counter.

"You didn't have to do that," Lydia says to me as she sits back down on the stool.

"Yes, I did. You're pregnant Lydia, and you need to make sure that everything is okay." I would never forgive myself if I just let her sit here and not get checked over. My gaze wanders to Brad, who is stood behind Lydia. I rub Lydia's back as she takes a sip of her drink.

"Thanks for that Brad. That guy was a real asshole," I say to him, giving him an appreciative smile for his help.

"No problem. Although, I have to say, you are definitely one feisty chick," he says, chuckling.

"Just looking out for my friend."

"Remind me never to piss you, or your friends, off." He smiles at me and then turns his attention to Lydia. "Does it hurt anywhere?" he asks, and it is at this moment that I remember that he is a fucking doctor.

"Not really," she replies. We don't get to continue the conversation as Paul comes striding over, his eyes wide with worry. He clearly broke several speed limits to get here as it has only been about two minutes since I spoke to him. He envelopes Lydia in his arms and helps her up off of the stool. He promises to let me know what the hospital says, and then he whisks her away, leaving me feeling helpless as I stare after my friend. I hope that everything is okay. I bite my lip and realise that I need to do everything I can to make Lydia's job safe whilst she is with child. Brad sits down on the stool that Lydia has just vacated. He goes to order a beer, but I stop him. I make my way around the bar and pull a bottle of beer out of the fridge. I open it and place it in front of him.

"On the house," I say, feeling like I need to thank him.

"Thanks," he says as he takes a swig of the drink. "So, anything else need doing around here, seeing as you seem keen to hand out free beers?" I laugh at his comment and shake my head.

"Not right now. You just relax and revel in the fact that you are the hero of the moment." My attention is diverted away from him by my phone ringing. "Excuse me," I say as I pull my phone from my pocket and answer the call.

"Hey babe," I say as I see that Jake is the one calling me.

"Hi gorgeous. How's things going at The Den?" he asks me. I spoke to him briefly earlier and told him that my head was fried from all of the paperwork that I had to catch up on.

"It's okay, well it was until five minutes ago. Lydia has just been taken to hospital."

"Why?"

"Some drunken idiot shoved into her. I called Paul and he came to get her. They left a few moments ago. I figured it was better for her to get checked out than leave it and then something happens later on."

"Shit. I hope she's okay."

"Me too. Paul said that he would let me know."

"Maybe I should give him a call or something?" Jake says.

"I think that might be a good idea," I reply, knowing how much I need my friends in times of turmoil. It may be just what Jake needs to do to get Paul to speak to him again. "Anyway, it turns out that your brother is a bit of a hero right now."

"Brad?"

"Yeah. The guy that knocked into Lydia was getting in my face, Brad showed up and put the guy on his ass." The line goes silent and I wonder if the call has been disconnected. "Jake?"

"Yeah, I'm still here." I hear him let out a sigh and I know that it is because Brad is here. I know how Jake's mind works. We may have all had fun the other night, but Jake still doesn't trust Brad. He especially doesn't trust Brad's intentions around me. "I'm coming to see you."

"Don't be silly Jake. You have had a long day."

"I don't care. I want to come and see you." I know that there is no point in arguing with him. He will come here now whether I tell him to or not.

"Okay. See you soon." I hang up the phone and place it back in my pocket. Jake and I had a long talk about Brad yesterday. Brad was a bit of a bastard towards Jake for years so it is hardly surprising that he is wary of him.

"Everything okay?" Brad asks me, downing the rest of his beer.

"Yeah. All good. Jake's on his way here now."

"He's pissed that I'm here and he's not, isn't he?" Brad asks me. I sigh and decide not to sugar coat my answer.

"Can you really blame him?" I say, raising my eyebrows at him.

"I guess not." He looks sad as he answers, and I feel a little bad that I am having this conversation with him, but my loyalty lies with Jake.

"You did some shitty things to him when you guys were younger. You just need to give him some time to get used to you being here again. If you want to be part of his life, then you need to show him that you have changed. You need to gain his trust back, and that is going to take more than a few days to achieve." Brad looks surprised by my words.

"You don't beat around the bush do you?" he says and I shrug my shoulders at him.

"What's the point in pussy footing around?" Brad smirks at me and I see his shoulders relax a little.

"See, feisty," he says as he nods in my direction.

"I fight tooth and nail for the people that I love, and Jake is one of those people." My hands are braced on the bar counter and Brad moves his hand so that it covers mine. I still at his movement.

"Jake is lucky to have met you." His voice is so quiet that I almost don't hear him. I pull my hand away, feeling a little uncomfortable. Unsure of what to say, I let my eyes drift past Brad and I see that Jake is walking over to us. I smile and busy myself pouring him a scotch. I figure that he needs something a little stronger than a beer to put him at ease. Jake reaches the bar counter and leans towards me, placing a kiss on my lips. As he takes a seat, next to Brad on one of the bar stools, I place his drink in front of him.

"Thanks," he says as he picks up his drink and takes a sip.

"I like to look after my favourite customers," I say with a wink before I go to help Susie serve drinks to a group of students.

Jake.

As I sit and sip the glass of scotch that Stacey had waiting for me when I arrived, I watch her behind the bar as she busies herself with serving customers. She is wearing her skinny jeans, which hug her ass allowing me to see her curves, a white figure-hugging t-shirt, and her come fuck me black work boots. I watch as she commands the bar, running it efficiently and smoothly whilst keeping the customers happy. Out of the corner of my eye, I notice that Brad is watching her also. I feel my jaw clench. I rip my gaze from Stacey and turn my head to look at him. He must notice my movements as he fidgets on his seat and turns to face me.

"What are you doing here Brad?" I ask him, wanting to know his reasons for being here.

"Enjoying a drink bro. Why else would I be here?" he answers cockily. I finish the rest of my scotch and place the glass back on the bar.

"I don't know," I answer honestly. I have a fair idea of why he might have come here, but I am trying to be reasonable and put my thoughts to one side.

"Listen bro, I have no hidden agenda here. I finished work and fancied a beer. I didn't want to go back to my room at the bed and breakfast, so I thought that I would come here." At this point, Stacey comes over, replacing my empty scotch glass with a full one. She winks at me and then returns to the other end of the bar. "She's a good one," Brad says, nodding in Stacey's direction.

"Yes, she is."

"So, tell me, how did you two meet?" he asks me. I don't particularly want to tell him the ins and outs, so I keep my answer short and simple.

"We met here actually."

"Wow, don't go overboard with the details," Brad says, sarcastically.

"I don't really see what business it is of yours," I answer, to which I hear Brad sigh loudly.

"I was just asking. Seeing as we have been getting on okay recently, I thought that I might get the chance to know more about your life. You know, for most families, this would be a normal conversation."

"Most families don't fuck the other ones over." I can't help the bite to my words as I speak.

"Jesus Christ Jake, you gotta let that shit go man." Brad runs a hand through his hair and I stare at him. "I know that I have fucked up in the past. I don't know how many times I can say sorry for that." He takes a swig of his beer before continuing. "I know that you have bailed me out of plenty of situations in the past. I know that I have tried to fuck up every relationship that you have ever had. I know that you don't trust me, but I am telling you that I have changed. Believe me when I say that, moving to America showed me just how fucking lonely my life was." He looks down at the bar, a sad look crossing his face. If I hadn't been burned by Brad before, then this would be the point where I would feel sorry for him. "Just give me a chance bro." I look to Stacey who gives me a smile as she walks to the till. I know that she wants me to give Brad a chance. She lost most of her family when she was a child. I know that she doesn't want me to throw away the chance to mend fences with Brad. I think about how emotional she got when she first told me about losing her parents, and then, in later years, her nan. I know that, if I give Brad a chance to prove himself, then Stacey will be there for me every step of the way. There will always be a part of me that is expecting him to fuck up again, but, maybe it is time to let go of some of the resentment? I know that, even if he wanted to, he would never be able to take Stacey from me. There is nothing he could do, or say, that would make her turn her back on me. If there is some master plan behind his insistence to mend our broken relationship, then more fool him. As long as I have Stacey, I can get through anything.

"Okay," I say.

"Okay?" Brad says, looking a little confused by my answer.

"One more chance Brad."

"Seriously?" he says, shock evident in his voice and on his face.

"Seriously." I give a nod of my head and then pick up my fresh glass of scotch. I sip the contents and I see Brad down the remainder of his beer. As his eyes settle back on Stacey, I make a promise to myself. I promise that, if he ever does anything to show his true colours, then I will be ready for him. Nothing mattered in my life when he screwed me over before, but now that I have something worth fighting for, he better be prepared to go to war.

Stacey.

I am exhausted by the time that Jake and I get back home. He stayed until I had closed up and had Eric pick us up and bring us home. Brad stayed until the end too and then made his own way back to the bed and breakfast. As I wearily get undressed and then make my way into the bed, Jake is already waiting for me. I pull the cover back and Jake envelopes me in his arms. We lie there and I relish in the feel of his warm body curled around mine. We talked in the limo about his conversation with Brad, and I am glad that he is going to give him a chance to make things right between them. I know that Jake is still wary, but he is willing to try, and that is all that matters. I would give anything to have some family left around me, and I think that might have played a part in Jake's decision. I just hope that Brad is true to his word, and that he really does want to put the past behind them. As I snuggle myself against Jake's body, I close my eyes and feel peace wash over me. My worries about Lydia were put to rest tonight when she text me to say that the doctor had checked her over and had said that she was fine. I told her that I would give her a call tomorrow and see how she is doing. I need to come up with a plan for her to be kept out of harm's way during her pregnancy whilst she is at work. I feel Jake place a kiss on my shoulder as sleep starts to claim me.

With the rollercoaster that we have been on in the last couple of months, I figure that this is our time for everything to run smoothly. Jake and I deserve happiness, and I will do everything in my power to make sure that we don't let the actions of others ruin that.

Chapter Twenty-Four.

Stacey.

Jake has already left for work by the time that I wake up. I have the day at home, before I go to The Den tonight for the evening shift. After catching up on all of the paperwork yesterday, I decide that today I will blitz the house and give it a clean. I get dressed in a pair of leggings and a long sleeved top and put my hair up. I make my way downstairs, my mobile phone in hand, and I make myself a coffee. I sit at the kitchen island and, as I wait for my coffee to cool, I give Lydia a call.

"Morning babes," she says as she answers the phone.

"Morning Lyd. How are you feeling this morning?" I ask her.

"Oh, I'm fine, and so is the little jellybean."

"Jellybean?"

"Yeah, jellybean." She chuckles and I laugh along with her.

"Well, I'm glad that the jellybean and yourself are okay."

"Me too, and despite my insistence that I am okay, Paul has taken the day off. He's currently making me some breakfast whilst I lie in bed. Honestly, he's more dramatic than me!"

"Uh, I doubt that Lyd," I say, laughing.

"Shush you. Anyway, how did the rest of your shift go?" she asks me.

"No problems. Brad stuck around until closing, and Jake showed up when I told him that Brad was there."

"Oh dear. Do I sense trouble?" Lydia knows bits about Brad and Jake's history, but she doesn't know all of it. Hell, I still don't think that I know the half of it. My knowledge of the situation stretches to knowing that Brad has always needed Jake to help him out, mostly with money, and of course the fact that Brad went off with the woman Jake was seeing before he went to America.

"Well, Jake says that he is willing to give Brad a chance, and I support him in that decision."

"I guess that only time will tell, huh?"

"I guess so."

"So, now that Jake and Paul are speaking again, can we discuss you guys coming round on Thursday night?" Lydia asks me.

"Well, I guess it couldn't hurt." I haven't actually spoke to Jake yet about how things went down with Paul when he phoned him last night to check on Lydia.

"Fantastic! Come round for seven and I will cook." I can hear how excited she is, and I hope that this turns out to be a good idea.

"We can talk about your new role at work then too."

"New role?" she asks.

"Yes, but I'm not discussing it now. I will speak to you about it on Thursday. In the meantime, you are off work with full pay." I don't want her to worry about her finances at a time like this. The last thing that she needs is to be stressing about money.

"But...."

"No buts Lydia. As your boss, I order you to take time off and relax."

"Uh, if you're sure?" she sounds a little hesitant, but I think that it is best for her to have some time off.

"Of course I'm sure." I can hear Paul speaking in the background and I presume that he is bringing her her breakfast. "Now, you enjoy your breakfast and get some rest."

"Thanks Stace. I'll give you a text later."

"Love ya Lyd."

"Love you too babes." The phone goes dead and I place it on the kitchen island and pick up my, now cooled down, coffee. I finish my drink quickly and decide to get cracking on the housework so that I can get it done and out of the way. I go to the hall way and open the cleaning cupboard, taking the hoover out and taking it into the lounge. I pop a CD into the stereo, turning the volume up full when Formation by Beyoncé starts playing. I plug the hoover in and begin to clean, singing and dancing to the music at the same time. The time passes quickly, and before I know it, I have cleaned the whole lounge. With the hoovering, polishing, and the fluffing of cushions done, I move into the kitchen. I start cleaning the worktops and Try Me by Jason Derulo starts playing. I flick the coffee machine on and make myself another cup whilst I dance to the beat of the music. Of course, when Jennifer Lopez starts to sing on the track, I think that I have morphed into her. I sing and dance around the kitchen as if my life depends on it. I shimmy the cloth along the worktops, lost in my own little world. When the song winds down and I stop shaking my hips, the sound of someone clapping behind me makes me scream. As I am screaming, I whirl around and see that Brad is stood in the kitchen doorway. He's grinning at me, but I am too shocked at seeing him standing there to register any words that he might be saying. My heart literally jumped into my throat when I heard him clapping behind me. I try to calm my erratic breathing, feeling irritation build up within me. I feel my face form into a scowl as my mind wonders what the hell he is doing here.

"Brad," I say breathlessly, once I have managed to get my mouth to form words. "What the hell is wrong with you? You almost gave me a heart attack!"

"Sorry. I didn't mean to scare you." He doesn't look too apologetic though if the smirk on his face is anything to go by.

"How did you get in here?" I ask.

"Through the front door funnily enough," he responds sarcastically. *I didn't unlock the front door. How in the hell did he open it? Maybe Jake left it unlocked?*

"Haven't you heard of knocking?" I say loudly, as another song starts to play making it impossible to talk at a normal level.

"I did knock, but clearly you couldn't hear me. Do you even have ear drums Stace?" he shouts, chuckling at the same time. I huff and walk past him, going to the lounge to turn the music off. I walk back to the kitchen and see that Brad has made himself comfy on one of the stools at the kitchen island.

"What are you doing here anyway?" I ask, my tone a little bit harsher than intended.

"Well, I just wanted to see if you fancied grabbing some breakfast." He says it so innocently, as if we do this kind of thing on a regular basis. Thoughts of how he got in here fly from my head at his suggestion.

"Me?"

"Yes Stace, you."

"But, why?" I am more than a little confused as to why he would want to get breakfast with me.

"I just thought that, with Jake deciding to give me a chance to make things up to him, that it would be a good idea to get to know you better. You are the most important person in his life after all."

"Um……." I have no idea what to say. I don't want to offend him, but I know that Jake wouldn't be comfortable knowing that I was out with Brad. I feel awkward, something that Brad obviously picks up on.

"Don't worry Stace. I get it," he says, looking a little downcast as he speaks. "I guess Jake wouldn't be happy with me taking you out. I'm sorry, it was stupid of me to ask you." I rack my brains for something to say, but there is nothing. If Brad had been in Jake's life when I first met him, then I am sure that this wouldn't even be an issue. But, Brad wasn't here back then.

"Hey," I say quietly to get Brad's attention. He looks up at me from under his lashes. "It's a nice thought and all, but I think that you need to give Jake more time to get used to you being around before you suggest anything like this. You just need to be patient. It won't be easy, but, it will be worth it in the end." I smile and hope that my words have softened the blow of me not taking him up on his offer. "Maybe we could all go out for drinks this weekend?" *In a neutral setting with plenty of other people around,* I add silently in my head.

"Will Martin be there?" He looks a little scared at the thought, and I laugh out loud. Martin really did put his personality on full display for Brad. It was hilarious to witness.

"I'm sure that he will be if he knows that you're going to be there. He has taken a shine to you," I say with a wink. He seems to relax at my comment and he starts to smile.

"Yes, he told me as much."

"I'm sure he did," I say, barely containing my laughter.

"Listen Stace," he says, his tone turning serious. "I just wanted to say thank you to you."

"What for?" I ask, truly perplexed as to why he would be thanking me.

"For trying to help me. I know that you are the reason that Jake is tolerating having me around." I have no answer for him. I just nod my head and smile at him. "Anyway, I guess I should be going. I don't want Jake to have any reason to cut me out, and I guess by being here, that is a possibility." I think he is hoping that I won't tell Jake that he showed up here unannounced, but I can't promise him that. I have no intention of hiding this from Jake.

"Jake will be fine," I tell him, not believing my words for one minute. "I will get him to call you about drinks at the weekend," I say as I walk him to the front door.

"Thanks Stace. Take care," he says as he leaves and I shut the front door behind him. I let out a long breath of air and lock the front door. I go upstairs to get washed and changed, needing to go and see Jake straight away. I take a quick shower and pick out some clothes to wear. I put on my black, bootcut trousers, a purple fitted top and my shoe boots. I redo my hair and put it back into a ponytail, and I apply a light touch of make-up. I am not looking forward to telling Jake about Brad, but I know that it has to be done, and there is no way that I want to tell him what just happened over the phone. With adrenaline pumping through me, I make my way out of the house and to my car to drive to Jake's office.

Jake.

"Mr Waters, Miss Paris is here to see you," Valerie tells me through the intercom on my desk.

"Send her through Valerie." I sit back in my office chair and I watch the doors to my office. Stacey walks in a few seconds later, looking as delicious as ever. My cock starts to twitch, something it does every time I lay my eyes on this woman. She walks around my desk and I turn my chair around so that she can sit on my lap.

"Hi handsome," she purrs before giving me a quick kiss on the lips. Even the sound of her voice gets my juices flowing. I put my arms around her and hold her against my body. I pull her head down to me, the first kiss not being long enough. She opens her mouth, allowing my tongue to massage with hers. I hold the nape of her neck in place, and only when I feel that I have had my fill of her, do I loosen my grip. She pulls back slightly and smiles. "I hope that you don't greet all of your visitors in that way Waters," she says in a teasing tone.

"Of course not. I only reserve this type of treatment for special guests." She chuckles and I love that we can have a bit of banter without her becoming needy or offended by my comments. “To what do I owe the pleasure of this unexpected visit?” An unexpected visit that I most definitely welcome.

“Well, I, uh..... I have something to tell you,” she says looking downwards, instantly putting me on edge. I know this woman’s body language better than she does, and I know that she doesn’t feel comfortable with whatever it is that she needs to tell me.

“What’s wrong Stace?”

“Why would there be anything wrong?”

“I know you, and I know that something is bothering you.” I can see the worry in her eyes as she places her hands on my chest and takes a deep breath.

“You have to promise me that you won’t get mad at what I am about to tell you.”

“That’s not exactly a great way to start the conversation babe.”

“Well I’m not telling you until you promise,” she says, stubbornly. I study her face and I know that she is not willing to budge on this condition. If I want to know what is bothering her, then I need to keep my cool.

“I promise,” I tell her. “Now what is it?”

“Brad came to the house just now.” My body tenses at her words, but I remain silent so that she can continue to speak. “He came by to ask me to go out to breakfast with him.” My jaw clenches with each word that she speaks. *What the fuck is he playing at?* "I told him no obviously," she says hurriedly. "He figured that by taking me out, he could thank me."

"Thank you for what?" I interrupt.

"He seems to think that the only reason that you are giving him a chance is because of me. He really does seem like he wants to build bridges with you Jake."

"There's building bridges though Stace and then there is just going one step too fucking far." I can't help but be pissed off that he even suggested the idea of taking her out.

"That's why I said no. Obviously I think that it would be good for you two to be on good terms again, but I would never jeopardise us by doing something that I know would upset you." God, this woman is incredible. She gets me. She understands what makes me tick. I lean forward and place a gentle, tender kiss on her lips.

"What was that for?" she asks, her eyes sparkling, the tension visibly leaving her body.

"Just because." I really didn't think that I could love her any more than I already do, but I guess that I can. "Thank you for telling me."

"You're welcome. I must say though, you are a lot calmer about this than I was expecting."

"I promised you that I wouldn't get mad, so I'm not." *Not on the outside anyway.*

"I said to him that we could go for drinks at the weekend, if you wanted to. He then looked a little scared about the fact that Martin could possibly be invited along." She laughs at the last bit and a smile crosses my lips.

"I think that Martin should definitely be invited."

"I thought that you might say that. Is Martin in today?" she asks me.

"Yeah. He was out this morning scouting out a possible location for the summer ball, but he should be back by now."

"Great. I'll stop by his office before I leave." She places a quick kiss on my cheek and then jumps off of my lap. "Don't forget that I am working tonight so I will be home late again."

"I know," I say, giving her a playful pout in response. She rolls her eyes at me and starts to make her way to the office door. She stops before opening it and turns back to me. "Hey Jake?"

"Mmmm?"

"Did you lock the front door this morning when you left for work?"

"Of course I did. Why?"

"Oh, no reason. I'll see you tonight, if you're awake."

"Oh I will be awake, don't you worry about that." She gives me her radiant smile and then closes the office door behind her. Questions run through my head about what the hell Brad thinks he is playing at by going to my house and asking Stacey to go out with him. But there is one question that is burning at the front of mind more than any others. *Why in the world would she ask me about locking the front door?*

Chapter Twenty-Five.

Stacey.

I manage to sneak out of work early as it is pretty quiet tonight. I leave Darren, Susie and Stephanie to it and I drive myself back home. I haven't told Jake that I am coming home as I want to surprise him. I pull onto the driveway to see that the house is in darkness and there is no sign of Jake's car. I exit the car and go to the front door, unlocking it. As I enter, I put the hall way light on and then lock the door behind me, straining my ears for any indication that Jake may have decided to get Eric to drive him home. The house is completely silent, so I shrug my shoulders, take my shoes off and make my way to the kitchen. I proceed to pour myself a glass of white wine which I then take upstairs with me. I enter our bedroom and take my wine through to the ensuite. A nice relaxing bath sounds like heaven right now, seeing as Jake isn't here to occupy my time. I begin to run the bath and put the wine on the side so that I can undress. I put in an obscene amount of bubbles, and inhale the lavender scent as the water continues to fill the bath tub. I leave the ensuite door slightly ajar so that I can hear when Jake gets home. I strip off my clothes, leaving them in a pile on the floor and I finish running the bath. As I get into the tub, goose-bumps rise on my skin from the welcoming heat. I sit back and take a sip of my wine as I try to relax, but it has been bugging me all day about how Brad got in here this morning. I believe Jake when he says that he locked the door, but that doesn't explain how Brad got in here.

With a weary sigh, I slide further down the bath tub so that the bubbles are touching my chin. I could mention my concerns to Jake, but I don't want to give him even more doubts over Brad than he already has. Then again, I don't want to piss him off by not telling him seeing as I promised myself that I would never keep anything from him again after the abortion leaflets misunderstanding. I close my eyes and will my brain to switch off for a while. I need to stop obsessing over something so trivial……

Jake.

By the time I return to my house, it is just gone half past nine. I decided that it was time that I just went round to Paul's and spoke to him, face to face. We have been friends for a long time, and I think of him as more of a brother than I do Brad. I caught him just before he was about to leave to go and see Lydia. I may have spoken to him on the phone, when Lydia had to go to hospital, but speaking on a phone is different to speaking in person. To start with, I thought he was going to tell me to fuck off, but he didn't. He invited me inside and offered me a beer, which I declined due to driving. I didn't want to keep him from Lydia, so I got straight to the point. Once I asked him what was wrong, he let me have it. He shouted at me about how I handled the whole abortion situation, and I let him rant and rave at me. He was pissed that I had made Lydia feel as though she had to speak up and tell him the truth in front of others. He was pissed at how I had treated

Stacey, knowing that it had made Lydia worry about her. I apologised to him, told him that he could hit me if that made him feel better, but he decided against that. Once he was done shouting at me, he seemed to relax more. I think that he needed to tell me what an asshole I had been, and I completely agreed with him. He needed to rant at me, face to face, in order to feel better. He then told me that Lydia had invited Stacey and I over to her place on Thursday night for dinner, and that he hoped that we would both be there. We shook hands before I left, and now I presume that it will all go back to normal again. As I pull onto the drive, I see Stacey's car parked there and the lights on in the house. *Huh? She must have been able to get off of work early.* I waste no time in getting out of the car and making my way inside the house. I make sure the front door is locked behind me, Stacey's question from earlier about locking the front door bugging me, and I race upstairs to see where she is. As I enter our bedroom, I see that the ensuite door has been left ajar. I quietly walk over and peek inside to see that Stacey is led in the bath, her head facing away from me. I push the door open some more and quietly step into the room. I watch her as she lies there peacefully. I can't see any of her body, other than her head, as she has a ridiculous amount of bubbles filling the bathtub. I tip toe across the room so that I am just behind her, and am about to lean down and place a kiss on her lips, when she startles me by speaking.

"I know that you're there Waters," she says as she opens her eyes and stares up at me with those captivating blue pools of hers. "Why are you creeping about the place?" she says with a cheeky smile.

"I wasn't creeping," I reply.

"You so were."

"Would you prefer it if I was to creep somewhere else?" I ask, enjoying the easy flow of banter between the two of us.

"No. I would prefer it if you could undress yourself quickly and creep into this bath tub with me." She raises one eyebrow and her tongue runs along her bottom lip. I don't need to be asked twice. I strip my clothes off, leaving them on top of hers on the floor, and I jump into the bath tub, making some of the water and bubbles splash onto the floor. "Jake!" she shrieks as water splashes her face and bubbles fly into the air. I laugh and pull her against me, angling her face and moving her closer so that I can feel her lips on mine. She straddles me as her legs go either side of my hips, her sex hovering just above my, now hard, cock. My hands roam up and down her back, sliding against her smooth skin. I can feel her nipples harden against my chest, and I love how I have the power to turn her on so much. I do that to her. Me. Her hands move to the tops of my thighs and my cock gives a twitch at her hands being so close. She glides her palm across my thigh and wraps her fingers around the bottom of my cock. I break my lips from hers and I take in her glazed eyes and flushed cheeks.

"Are you sure that you don't want me to creep away?" I whisper to her, teasingly.

"No way Waters," she says against my lips, running her tongue along my bottom lip making my body tingle. I watch her as she lowers herself onto my cock, taking me all the way. She slowly begins to rise and fall, making each plunge inside of her deliciously torturous. I take her nipple into my mouth and suck, causing her to groan loudly. Her hands fly to my head, holding me against her breast. I flick her nipple with my tongue and then move to the other breast to repeat my actions. I feel Stacey tighten around me, and it makes me want to take charge, but I don't. It's always hard for me to hold back and let her control our movements. I will never get enough of her. She speeds up slightly as her body shudders, and I know that she is close to her release. I place my thumb over her clit, and I move it in small circles. Her eyes connect with mine and she whispers my name. I hold the nape of her neck to stop her from looking away from me. I love watching her come. It's the most erotic thing that I have ever seen. My release is building slowly, and I remove my hand from her clit so that we can reach our heights at the same time. With her hips grinding, and her breathing becoming laboured, her movements become quicker. Just when I think that she is about to come, she lifts herself up and slams down on me, causing my release to rush to the surface. I call out her name as she slams down on me again and then I am unfolding inside of her. She cries out on the third slam and I feel her convulse around me, making my climax more intense. She moves one last time, and then her body collapses on top of mine. I hold her shaking body close, and bury my face in her neck as I catch my breath. Stacey lets her hands run up and down my arms, sighing with satisfaction.

"Now that is much better," she says against my ear.

"So I take it that I am free to creep about the place in future then?"

"If it results in pleasure like that every time, then feel free to creep about all you like Mr Waters."

Chapter Twenty-Six.

Stacey.

Jake and I are sat at the dining table, enjoying a cooked breakfast that I made for us before we both have to go to work. As I finish my food, I pick up mine and Jake's cups and make us another coffee. When I return Jake has finished eating and is looking at his phone.

"Thanks," he says as I place his cup of coffee in front of him. I resume my place on the other side of the table and sit back in the chair.

"Everything okay over there?" I ask him, seeing that his brows are furrowed.

"Yeah," he replies, placing his phone on the table. I raise one eyebrow at him to question his answer and he sighs. "I tried to phone Brad yesterday and got no reply about going for drinks Saturday night. I also sent him a message about it, but he hasn't got back to me yet."

"Okay," I say slowly, wondering why Jake is worrying over Brad not texting him back. "Maybe he's just busy with work or something?"

"Hmmmm."

"Oh, I forgot to tell you that Lydia has invited us over for dinner on Thursday night," I say, diverting the conversation away from any mention of Brad.

"I know, Paul told me. I went to see him last night, before you had your wicked way with me in the bath tub." He winks at me and I smile at him, understanding why he never mentioned speaking to Paul before now. As soon as we got out of the bath and got dried, we went to bed and as soon as my head hit the pillow, I fell asleep.

"How was it when you saw him?"

"It was fine. He told me what had pissed him off and that's it." He shrugs his shoulders and sips his coffee. It always amazes me that blokes can move on from things quickly. If only it was that easy for us women.

"So, you're okay with going round there on Thursday?"

"Yeah."

"Okay then." My phone beeps to alert me to a text and I see that Martin has replied to the message that I left him yesterday. I stopped by his office after seeing Jake yesterday, but he wasn't there, so I sent him a text asking if he was free to come out on Saturday night.

Hell yeah I'm free! What's the plan?

Martin x x

I send a text back informing him that I will pick him up and he can come to my house for drinks beforehand. Martin is yet to see where I live, so I figure it's about time that I show him around the place. I get a reply from him seconds later, and it seems that he can barely contain his excitement at coming to see the house. I laugh at his reply and Jake looks at me, clearly wondering what has made me chuckle.

"Martin is coming out on Saturday with us. It seems he is a little bit excited about me inviting him here first."

"Oh lord, he's going to inspect the place with a fine-tooth comb, isn't he?"

"Probably," I say, smiling.

"Listen, I have been thinking," Jake says, changing the subject. "I know that we talked about going away a while ago, but we haven't sorted out any dates yet."

"Well, I guess we could do something in a couple of months' time?" I say, not really wanting to up and leave when I haven't long gone back to work.

"A couple of months? I was hoping we could go before that."

"It's a nice thought Jake, but I can't take time off from work again. I've only been back there a few days as it is, and I need to start interviewing people, to employ someone to take Lydia's place. There is no way that she can work the bar after what happened to her the other day." Jake sighs in frustration. I reach across the table and place my hand on his. "I would love nothing more than for us to get away for a break, but, right now, it just isn't feasible." I give his hand a little squeeze and he gives me a slight smile. I know that he is disappointed with my answer, but he can't expect me to drop everything, just like I wouldn't have thought that he would be able to with his business. I stand up, picking my plate and cup up at the same time so that I can load them into the dishwasher. When I return to the table to get Jake's plate, he grabs my hand and turns so that he is facing me. I look down at him and am instantly captivated by his caramel pools.

"You are such a stubborn woman," he says in a low voice.

"I prefer the term assertive to stubborn," I reply with a shrug of my shoulders. He laughs and I smile at the sound that it makes. He stands up and his tall frame means that I have to tilt my head slightly to look at him.

"You know, when we do go away, it's going to be the best fucking holiday ever. Just the two of us. Work always used to come first in my life, but all that has changed. You come first now and I can't wait to spend some time away from reality with you." *How does he always know just the right things to say?*

"You know it's my birthday in a couple of months' time?"

"Yes Stace, I know when your birthday is." He furrows his brow, clearly not seeing why I am bringing this up.

"Well, why don't we go away then?"

"Really?"

"Yes. Really." I smile at him and a warmth spreads through me at the grin that spreads across his face.

"Done. I will book it today. Anywhere in particular you want to go?" he asks me, looking ridiculously excited.

"Surprise me," I whisper. He cups my face in his hands and brings his lips to mine. My phone ringing interrupts our embrace and we both groan in unison at having to pull apart. I walk to the kitchen island and see that Lydia is calling me.

"Good morning Lyd. How's things?" I say as I answer the phone.

"Uh, are you free for a chat this morning?" she sounds a little nervous.

"What's wrong?"

"Nothing. I just need to speak to you. Can you come round to mine?"

"Okay. I can be with you in ten minutes."

"Great. I will have the coffee waiting." She clicks the phone off and I wonder why she sounds so cagey.

"I have to go," I say to Jake. "Lydia needs to see me."

"Is she okay?"

"I don't know as she didn't say much. I hope that nothing is wrong with the baby." I grab my handbag and give Jake a quick kiss. "What time will you be home?" I ask him.

"Not sure. I have a meeting at three this afternoon which could go on for a while."

"Okay, well, I will see you later then." I am not down to work tonight so at least we will be able to spend some time together. I start to walk from the room, only to be stopped by Jake calling my name. I stop walking and turn to look at him.

"Let me know how Lydia is when you have spoken to her."

"Will do."

"I love you."

"Love you too," I say as I blow him a kiss. I rush out of the front door to my car and hope to god that Lydia is okay.

Chapter Twenty-Seven.

Stacey.

I get to Lydia's and she ushers me into her flat, and through to her lounge. I take a seat on the sofa and see that she has coffee and biscuits laid out on the table. Lydia sits on the chair opposite me and I stare at her, waiting for her to speak.

"Thanks for coming round," she says.

"No problem. Now, what's the matter?" I don't beat around the bush.

"Paul has asked me to move in with him," she says quietly. It takes me a few moments to answer her. I thought that she was going to tell me some bad news, but from what I can see, this is a good thing.

"Okay," I say slowly. "And that is a bad thing because?" She's going to have to help me out here as I am a little lost as to why she looks so downcast.

"Oh my gosh, I don't even know where to start." She sounds exasperated as she speaks. "Do you not think that it is too soon? What if I move in with him and everything goes to shit? My track record with men isn't great. What if I do something to mess our relationship up? What if I live with him and he decides that he doesn't want me anymore?" Lydia is rambling so fast that I almost can't keep up with her.

"Lyd, slow down. One question at a time."

"Sorry. I guess I'm just freaking out a little."

"A little? I would say that you are freaking out a lot," I point out to her. She puts her head in her hands and sighs.

"I just, I don't want to screw this up. I love Paul, and I don't want to do something to make him hate me."

"Why on earth would you ever make him hate you?"

"This is me Stace," she says, her voice rising a little. "Nothing ever runs smoothly with me. I just keep thinking that, one day, Paul is going to wake up and wonder what the hell he ever saw in me." She has tears in her eyes when she looks at me, and my heart goes out to her.

"Stop that right now," I say firmly. "Stop putting yourself down Lydia. Paul loves you, and he just wants to be with you. You guys are having a baby together for goodness sake."

"Exactly. What if he is just asking me because of the baby?" *Oh jeez!*

"Lydia, you need to calm down and take a breath." She actually does take a deep breath as she looks to me for answers. "Paul wouldn't ask you to move in if he didn't want you with him. You need to have more faith in yourself. Yes, you have had the misfortune of being with men who are assholes, but is there anyone who hasn't?" She doesn't answer me, but I can see that she is thinking about what I am saying. "Plus, you're going to be a little family in the near future. Do you really want to live in separate places when the baby is here?"

"I guess not," Lydia says.

"And, who is to say that it is too soon? What happened to the hopeless romantic that is my best friend?"

"She got wise."

"Well, maybe she needs to remain wise but let that romantic spark back in. You deserve to be happy."

"Do you think?" she still sounds uncertain, but she doesn't look as downcast as she did when I first arrived here.

"Yes. Don't let your past experiences affect what you have now."

"Hmmm."

"Do you not think that maybe, there is the slight possibility that your hormones are all over the place right now?"

"No. Why would my hormones have anything to do with this?" Lydia says, jumping on the defence rather quickly.

"Well you are pregnant, as if that isn't stating the obvious, so you could just be overthinking things due to being hormonal."

"Well I'm not," Lydia replies matter of factly. "You sound just like Paul. He said the same thing to me last night when I got annoyed that he hadn't picked a towel up off of the floor. I mean honestly, talk about an overreaction on his part." Lydia rolls her eyes and picks up a biscuit. I stifle a laugh as I hide my face behind my coffee cup. Yes, hormones are definitely playing a factor in all of this, but I am not going to be the one to argue that with her. If there is one thing that you should never do, it's to piss a pregnant woman off.

"Listen Lyd, whilst I'm here, I might as well tell you about the plan for work."

"The plan?"

"Yes. I thought that it would be a good idea for you to be paperwork based for the time being." I can see that she isn't overjoyed by this idea, but she needs to understand that she needs to be more careful now.

"Paperwork? But, it's so boring."

"Believe me, I know, but it wouldn't be forever." Lydia goes quiet and it is at this moment that I hear her front door opening and closing. I turn my head to look at the hall way and see Nick appear a few seconds later. He leans against the door frame, hands in his pockets and a big grin on his face.

"Morning ladies," he says looking smug.

"Morning Nick," I reply.

"Morning," Lydia says. "And I presume that the dopey look on your face is due to some piece of skirt that you spent the night with?" she asks him, not hiding the disgust in her voice.

"Oh come on sis, lighten up will you?" Nick says and I take that as my cue to leave.

"Lyd, I need to get to The Den. Think about what I said and I will speak to you later." I stand up and walk over to give her a hug before turning to leave the lounge. Nick is still leaning against the door frame and I have to squeeze past him as he clearly doesn't want to move.

"See ya later Stace," he says to my back as I walk towards the door. I wave without turning round and can hear Lydia shouting at him as I close the front door. With her moods all over the place, I don't envy Nick for the bollocking that I am sure she is giving him right now. I walk out of the building and head to my car, only for my attention to be grabbed by a white piece of paper under my wind screen wiper. I frown as I approach the car and take the piece of paper out. It is folded in half, so I unfold it to see what it says.

Just to let you know that I am missing you already.

xxxxxxx

My first thoughts immediately go to Jake. He would be the only one to leave me a note like this. I smile at his thoughtfulness, even though it would have been easier for him to just text or ring me. *He must have been passing by this way for a meeting or something.* I fold the note back up and place it on the passenger seat of the car as I sit in the driver's seat. I push all thoughts of nice notes and naughty thankyou's out of my head as I drive to work. I have a busy day ahead and I can't let myself be distracted. I am making today my mission to advertise for new bar staff.

Chapter Twenty-Eight.

Stacey.

I have no idea where the last few days have gone. It has been nothing but a whirlwind, what with setting things up ready to interview potential new staff members as well as doing my bar shifts at The Den. I have also been showing Lydia all of the paperwork side of the business which has added to my workload. I have barely seen Jake for the last few days. He has been busy trying to acquire another new deal, and by the time that I have arrived home from work, I am so tired that I have fallen asleep as soon as my head has touched the pillow. I am looking forward to tonight though. Jake and I are going to Lydia's flat for the evening and I can't wait to just unwind and spend some quality time with the people closest to me. As I sit at my desk, I let out a loud groan. Lydia looks at me and raises one of her eyebrows and allows a smirk to grace her face. She is sat next to me, at my desk, and has been helping me conduct interviews for the past two hours. The way that I am feeling right now, I would rather employ a couple of trained chimps than anyone that has walked through my office door.

"It's no good you smirking Lydia."

"Oh come on Stace, even you have to admit that the last guy we interviewed was funny." I think that Lydia may have taken leave of her senses for a moment, but then she bursts out laughing and I can't help but laugh along with her. The last guy we interviewed had said that he had previously worked at a hotel bar and had plenty of customer service skills. What he actually meant was that he had worked in a strip club some years ago, and by customer service skills, what he actually meant was that he knew how to spout cheesy chat up lines and that is about it.

"Okay, the situation was kind of funny, but the guy himself, not so much."

"You mean you didn't like his opening line of, 'baby, did you fall from heaven, or am I dead?'" Lydia says in a badly put on male voice before she erupts into more laughter, wiping away the tears streaming down her face.

"Ugh. I think it's fair to say that he fluffed the interview before he even sat down on that seat," I say, pointing to the chair on the other side of my desk.

"I'm so glad that you asked me to do the interviews with you. I needed a good laugh," Lydia says, finally calming down a little.

"Glad to be of service." I smile at her and am pleased to see that she seems more relaxed than she has been in a while. Lydia picks the list of names up off of the desk and starts to study it. "So, what's the name of the next potential candidate?" I ask her, leaning back in my chair and stifling a yawn. Lydia doesn't get a chance to answer as my office door opens, and Susie walks in with the next interviewee trailing behind her. Recognition washes over me as Susie steps to one side and Bonnie makes her way to the vacant chair on the other side of my desk. "Bonnie?" I screech, sitting bolt upright.

"Hey Stace. It's good to see you," she says cheerfully.

"Oh my god, it's been way too long since I last saw you," I say as I stand up and walk around the desk to give her a hug.

"It has. What happened to you? You always used to come to Danish for coffee, but then you just, stopped," Bonnie asks me as I gesture for her to sit down. I take my seat back behind my desk and give her an apologetic look.

"I'm sorry. Things have just been a little hectic lately. I have been meaning to come and see you, but, with running this place, I haven't had much spare time." It sounds like a lame excuse, but it is the truth. Things have been up and down for the last few months, but I don't have time to go into detail about it all now.

"Well, it would be nice to catch up with you when things aren't so crazy," Bonnie says, smiling.

"That would be good," I say as Bonnie and Lydia exchange hello's and how are you's. At the sight of Bonnie sat here, I suddenly feel hopeful. I know that Bonnie is a fantastic worker. She would be perfect for this place.

"So, shall we get on with the interview?" Lydia asks, placing the piece of paper in her hands down on the desk.

"Sure," I reply and I direct my attention back to Bonnie. "So, what happened with your job at Danish?"

"New owners happened. They weren't very accommodating with the shift patterns, so I had to leave. I have been looking for something a little different. I saw the advert for bar staff a couple of days ago and, hey presto, here I am."

"Well, do you know how to pour drinks, open bottles, and mix cocktails?" I ask her.

"Um, yes I can open bottles. I have poured pints at a previous bar job, but the only cocktails I have ever made have been the ones that I have prepared at home before a night out." She chews her lip nervously. I look to Lydia who is sat there with a big grin on her face. She knows that I always got on well with Bonnie, and she knows what a hard worker Bonnie is from all of our times of going to Danish. I think Lydia already knows what I am about to do.

"That sounds good enough to me. Cocktails are easy to learn. You're hired," I tell her. Bonnie's eyes go wide and Lydia starts nodding in agreement with me.

"Really? But, don't you want to ask me anything else?" Bonnie says, clearly surprised by my offer of employment.

"Trust us honey," Lydia says, "you are like a breath of fresh air in here today."

"It's true. Before you walked in, I had lost all hope," I say.

"I...... I don't know what to say," Bonnie says.

"Just say that you accept the job," I tell her.

"Yes. Yes, I accept."

"Fab! Your training will start on Saturday night. Be here for six o clock, and bring your relevant information so that I can get you on the payroll as soon as possible," I say, putting a great big tick next to her name on the list.

"Yes of course. Thank you so much girls. I'm so grateful."

"No problem. The dress code is pretty casual. Just smart jeans or trousers, and a black or white top will be fine, and a pair of black shoes or boots," I inform her.

"Okay," Bonnie says, still looking shocked.

"Great," I say standing up. Bonnie follows suit and I walk around the desk so that I can walk her to the office door. "We'll see you Saturday then."

"You sure will. Thank you," Bonnie says as she hugs me and then walks out to the main room where Susie will show her out. I close the office door behind her and breathe a sigh of relief.

"Thank god she walked in," Lydia says, mimicking my thoughts.

"I know. She has certainly brightened up the day. Who have we got next?" I ask as I make my way back to my seat.

"Larry Darlington," Lydia answers. The office door opens and Susie escorts a young man into the room. Susie makes a swift exit as the man takes a seat. Lydia's mouth drops open at the sight of Larry sitting before us. He has long pink dreadlocks, his t-shirt and jeans have rips everywhere, his face is covered in multiple piercings, and I can't see a scrap of skin that doesn't have a tattoo on it. I turn to look at Lydia and she catches my eye. I bite my lip to stop myself from laughing. I think it is safe to say that our afternoon may just be more interesting than our morning.

Jake.

I told Stacey that I would meet her at Lydia's due to my meeting finishing late. It's just gone seven by the time that I get to Lydia's flat, and I feel bad that I am so late for dinner. I know that Stacey has been looking forward to tonight, but a part of me wishes I could just have her to myself. The last few nights she has been exhausted when she has come home from work, and we have barely had any time to ourselves. I understand that she wants to prove that she can run The Den, but I really hope that the interviews she conducted today were a success. I miss my girl. As I knock on Lydia's front door, I can hear laughter inside. I smile as I hear Stacey laughing. The door is swiftly opened by Paul.

"Hey man," he says. "Come save me from the women. They have been talking in code ever since they got back from work. Whoever they interviewed today has sure given them some comedy value."

"I can hear them laughing from out here," I say as I enter the flat and take off my jacket. I hang it up by the door and follow Paul into the lounge. Lydia and Stacey are sat on the sofa, Stacey with her back to me, and Lydia is wiping tears from her face.

"Hi Jake," Lydia says, prompting Stacey to turn around and look at me. I nod to Lydia but my eyes are fixed on Stacey.

"Hi babe," she says. She stands up off of the sofa and comes over to give me a hug. I wrap my arms around her waist and pull her against me. I inhale her scent as I bury my nose in her hair. I place a kiss on the end of her nose and she smiles at me.

"Hi yourself," I reply as she steps out of my embrace and resumes her seat next to Lydia. She pats the sofa on the other side of her and I take that as my cue to sit down.

"Beer?" Paul asks me and I nod my head in response. He disappears into the kitchen and I turn my attention to the ladies, who are still chuckling away.

"How did the interviews go today?" I ask and am greeted with another round of laughter from them. Paul comes back into the room with my beer and he takes a seat in the chair.

"See what I mean? I can't get any sense out of them," Paul says, sitting back in the chair and sipping his own beer.

"Oh shush you," Lydia says. "If you had seen what we have today, then you would be laughing just as much as us."

"It's true," Stacey interrupts.

"Please tell me that you were able to hire someone?" I ask, needing her to tell me that she is going to lighten her workload.

"Actually, I hired two people."

"Seriously?" I ask her.

"Yeah. I'm not quite sure how I managed to get two mind as it was slim pickings all day long." Stacey reaches forward and picks up her glass of wine and takes a sip. I watch as the liquid wets her lips and I have to clench my teeth together so that my cock doesn't start to twitch at the mere sight. A beeping starts going off in the kitchen prompting Paul and Lydia to jump up at the same time.

"That's dinner ready. Give me a few minutes to dish up," Lydia says as she goes to exit the lounge. Paul follows her, ever the doting boyfriend. I can hear Lydia telling him that she is quite capable of dishing up the food by herself, but he doesn't come back to the lounge, so I presume that he is choosing to ignore her.

"So, if you hired two more people to work behind the bar, and Lydia is taking over the paperwork side of things, does this mean that I get you to myself a bit more?" I ask Stacey, pulling her closer to me. She slides onto my lap and links her hands behind my neck.

"Maybe," she teases as she lowers her lips to mine and kisses me. Her lips taste of the wine that she has been drinking, and she keeps the pressure minimal. She runs her tongue along my bottom lip and I have to remind myself that we are about to eat dinner with our friends.

"I can't wait to bury myself in you tonight Miss Paris." She bites her bottom lip which makes me want to bite it for her. It is at this moment that Lydia calls out to us that we can go through to the kitchen. Stacey chuckles and jumps off of my lap, holding her hand out to me. I take her hand and stand up, groaning a little that we have been interrupted so quickly.

"All in good time Waters. All in good time."

Chapter Twenty-Nine.

Jake.

I am led on the bed, flicking through the television channels, when Stacey walks out of the ensuite looking like a million fucking dollars. I have to physically stop myself from pouncing off the bed and ripping every piece of clothing from her body.

"See something that you like?" she asks me like the fucking minx that she is.

"Always," I reply honestly. My eyes roam over her, from head to toe, and I honestly think that this woman, somehow, manages to become more beautiful by the day. Before I can say anything else, the doorbell rings. Stacey squeals and makes a hasty exit from the bedroom. I make myself get off of the bed and go to the ensuite to get myself ready. I know that this is going to be Martin arriving, and as much as I like Martin, I know that he is going to be so dramatic about every detail of the house that I feel the need to hide for a little longer.

Stacey.

I run down the stairs and reach the ground floor, flinging the front door open to be greeted by the sight of Martin in the most outrageous outfit that I think I have ever seen him wear. A purple satin shirt, complete with billowing cuffs, red skinny jeans and a pair of blue dress shoes adorn his body.

"Baby girl," he says as he throws his arms around me and pulls me into a bear hug. When he steps back a few moments later, he looks me up and down and nods in approval. "Oh yes, I like it. Sexy black playsuit, check. Fuck me silver heels, check. Sexy, sleek hair, check. Dramatic make-up, check." I laugh at him and usher him inside. I give Eric a wave and beckon him over, but he politely declines and gets back into the driver's seat of the limo. Jake organised Eric picking Martin up tonight in the limo. I tried to object, but once Jake mentioned it to Martin there was no way that I was going to win that argument. As I close the front door, Martin has already started walking down the hall way so that he can start his inspection of the place. "Oh my god. This house is like a mini mansion," he exclaims as he enters the lounge.

"Don't exaggerate Martin." I roll my eyes at him.

"I'm not. Seriously, why the hell haven't I been invited here before now?" he asks as he collapses onto the sofa and sinks into the seat. "Wow. This sofa is like butter on your butt cheeks." He closes his eyes and lets out a loud sigh. I laugh in response and go to pull him off of the sofa so that we can go to the kitchen and get a drink. As I take hold of his hand he playfully swats at me. "Oh no, just two more minutes. This is bliss."

"Come on Martin. There will be plenty of other times for you to pamper your butt cheeks, but now isn't one of them." I pull on his hand and he reluctantly stands up.

"I seriously want to come for a sleepover."

"Fine. We will sort something out. Now can we please go and get a drink?"

"Sure." Martin is still gawping around the room as we go back into the hall way. Jake comes down the stairs at the same time as we enter the hall way. He looks divine in his dark denim jeans, ice blue shirt and black dress shoes. I swear, the man doesn't have to do anything to make himself look this good. I let my eyes rake over him and he grins at my obvious perusal of his body.

"Fucking unbelievable," Martin exclaims behind me, making me jump. "A limo, a gorgeous house, and you also have the perfect man in your life. Ugh. It's so not fair," he says as he flounces into the kitchen. Jake raises one eyebrow at me.

"Do I dare ask?" he says.

"Probably best not to," I advise him. "You look good Waters."

"Just good?" he says as he stalks towards me. I feel my heart beat speed up a notch.

"Okay, not just good. You look fucking hot." There is no point playing down how hot I think he looks. He can probably tell just by my body language alone anyway. He smirks as he backs me up against the wall.

"Just so you know," he whispers in my ear, his heated breath causing goose-bumps to rise on my skin. "All I have wanted to do, since you came out of the bathroom wearing that get up, is rip it off of you." His hands skim my sides and I shiver at his touch. I am about to retaliate when a squeal from the kitchen brings me back to reality. I gently shove Jake away from me and I rush into the kitchen to see if Martin is okay.

"What's wrong?" I ask Martin as I go and stand beside him, my eyes scanning everywhere to see why he squealed.

"Please tell me that you do not have a fucking hot tub in that garden?" he says comically, pointing to where the hot tub is situated.

"Um, okay. We don't have a hot tub in the garden," I say, sarcastically with a shrug of my shoulders.

"Don't play games with me baby girl. A hot tub to add to your list is just even more unfair. Ugh. I am staying here for a whole weekend. I don't just want one night, I want two." I laugh at his dramatics.

"Whatever you say Mart. Now, let me pour some drinks and then we can be on our way." I pull on his arm and drag him away from the sight of the hot tub. He sits on one of the stools, at the kitchen island, and watches as I pour us each a gin, lemonade and lime. I pop a straw into Martin's glass and hand it to him.

"Thanks baby girl." Jake walks into the kitchen just as I am finishing pouring him a scotch. I hand it to him and he places a kiss on the top of my head as he says thank you.

“Hey Jake,” Martin says.

“Yeah?”

“This house is the bomb.” I stifle a laugh at Martin’s description.

“Uh, thanks,” Jake replies, taking a healthy swig of his scotch. Martin asks if he can go and use the toilet, so I direct him to the one on the first floor. I know that he will be snooping for a good ten minutes before he returns, giving me enough time to finish my drink before we leave.

“Did Brad ever get back to you about tonight?” I ask Jake.

“Nope. I guess he must have found a new ‘hobby.’” I don’t fail to notice the sarcasm in Jake’s tone. I guess by ‘hobby’ he means woman.

“Oh well. His loss,” I say flippantly. I hear another squeal come from upstairs and I roll my eyes. “I better go and see what is making Martin squeal this time.” As I go to exit the kitchen, Jake stops me.

“Can I just ask, did I hear Martin say something about him staying here at some point?” Jake asks me, making me grin from ear to ear. “Oh god.” I laugh as I walk off and go in search of Martin and his screeching.

Chapter Thirty.

Stacey.

We arrive at The Den just before six o clock. Eric drops us off in the car park at the back as the place isn't open for customers yet. I let us in through the back door and I can already hear activity in the main room. Jake and Martin follow behind me as I head for the bar area, where Darren is currently trying to impress Bonnie by attempting to juggle with some lemons. Susie sees me and just rolls her eyes, and then goes back to getting things ready for opening time. As I reach the bar counter, I clear my throat loudly, making Darren drop the three lemons that he was using for his entertainment. He whirls around and has wide eyes as he sees me stood there. I'm not sure why he looks so petrified though, it's not like I am the strictest boss in the world.

"Sorry boss," Darren says as he scurries around on the floor to retrieve the lemons.

"Uh huh," I mumble as I look to Bonnie and see her trying to stifle a giggle. She has certainly dressed accordingly, which I knew that she would. She looks cute in black jeggings, black kitten heels and a white wrap around top. Her hair is pulled back into a high ponytail, and her minimal make-up allows her natural features to shine through.

"Is Tom not here yet?" I ask, to no one in particular.

"Who's Tom?" Susie says.

"He's the other new bar staff member."

"There's two new people?" Darren asks, still looking red faced from his lemon juggling disaster.

"Yes. Is that a problem?" I ask him.

"No. No problem."

"Don't worry Darren, I'm not replacing any of you guys." I see him physically breathe a sigh of relief at my words. Out of the corner of my eye, I see that Jake and Martin have taken a seat at the bar. Susie goes over to them and asks them what they want to drink. I don't even have to ask her to go over to them, she knows the drill. Darren goes to the back of the bar and finishes setting up the cocktail station. He doesn't ask who Jake and Martin are, but I do notice that he keeps glancing at them. No doubt he will be asking Susie about them when I am out of ear shot.

"Bonnie," I say, startling her. "We can't wait any longer for Tom. It's nearly opening time and I need to show you a couple of things before then."

"Okay," she says coming to stand beside me.

"We'll go through to my office and then I will show you where you can put your stuff," I say, indicating to her hand bag and coat.

"Cool."

"First though, there is someone that I would like you to meet." I smile at her and lead her over to Martin and Jake. "Obviously you know Martin from our trips to Danish so I don't need to introduce you to him."

"Hi Bon," Martin pitches in.

"And this is Jake Waters. He owns this place," I tell her. Her eyes go wide and she shifts on the spot. I guess she didn't expect to meet the owner on her first shift.

"Pleased to meet you," Jake says, ever the gentleman. He holds his hand out for her to shake, which she does.

"You too," Bonnie stammers.

"She forgot to mention that I am also her boyfriend," Jake says, nodding in my direction.

"I was just getting to that part," I say as I place my hands on my hips. "You'll have to excuse him Bonnie, he can be a little needy at times." Jake chuckles and I know that he has taken my comment at its comedy value. Bonnie smiles as she watches the easy banter between us.

"Oh please," Martin says as he sips his drink. "These two are just as bad as one another," he says, pointing at both me and Jake.

"Shush you," I say, smacking him playfully on the arm. I cut the conversation short because I don't have time to carry it on. I tell Jake and Martin that I need to show Bonnie a few things before we open and then I lead Bonnie to my office. We go through some forms and

Bonnie gives me her relevant information for the payroll. After that, I show her the staff room, which is Lydia's old office, and then I give her a quick rundown of the protocols expected. I show her the weekly rota, which is up on a noticeboard in the staff room. I have already added her name to it for the coming week. I take her back to the bar area and see that customers are already starting to filter in. There is still no sign of Tom, so I busy myself showing Bonnie the ropes. Darren is already busy making up cocktails and Susie is serving a couple of guys that have taken up residence at the bar. I see Jake's glass is empty, so I ask Bonnie to pour him a scotch and take it over to him. I decide that I should go and phone Tom to see where he is. I tell Bonnie that I will be back in a minute and I go to my office and close the door behind me. I walk to my desk and freeze on the spot when I see that there is a huge bouquet of flowers sitting in a vase on my desk. The flowers are beautiful and I can see a card poking out of the top. I take the card and open it.

Nowhere near as beautiful as you.

Hope you like them.

xxxxx

I smile as I read the note and I instantly forget to ring Tom as I rush back out to the bar to thank Jake for the flowers. I come up behind him and place my hands on his shoulders, leaning down so that my lips are by his ear.

“Thank you,” I say as move my body to the side of him so I can look at his handsome face.

“Thank you for what?” he asks me, looking genuinely confused. I know that Jake can put on an act when he wants to, so I take no notice of his confusion.

“For the flowers. They’re stunning.” I place a light kiss on his lips.

“What flowers?” I roll my eyes at him.

“The ones that are sat in my office. The ones that you had delivered here with this note,” I say, handing him the piece of card with writing on. He takes the card and reads it, but he doesn’t smile. In fact, he looks pissed off. Before I can say anything else, Jake grabs my hand and leads me out of the main room and back into my office. He closes the door behind us and looks over at my desk. He inspects the flowers as if they are omitting a nasty stench.

“I didn’t send you these Stacey.” His mouth sets into a line and I can see that he is clenching his jaw.

“You must have,” I reply, but I don’t sound so sure. “Who else would send me flowers?”

“Fuck knows, but it wasn’t me.” He walks over to the offending flowers and studies them like he is going to get answers from them. I wrap my arms around myself and start to feel uneasy. *If it wasn’t Jake, then who was it? Someone has obviously been in my office and I don’t know who the hell it is.* A sense of unease creeps through me. The last person to creep about this place was Caitlin. I know that it isn't her this time, but some of the same feelings resurface.

"The camera's," I say to Jake as I have a lightbulb moment. He turns to look at me, clearly understanding where I am going with this. He takes a seat at my desk and switches my laptop on. Thank god Jake had extra cameras installed after the Caitlin fiasco. Looking at the footage will hopefully show us who has been in here. Jake brings up the relevant programme and brings up the camera footage.

"So these weren't in here when you came in with Bonnie?" Jake asks me.

"No."

"So it has happened in last thirty minutes or so?"

"I guess so."

"Right. I'll go back and find you and Bonnie in here, and then we will just have to watch to see who came in here and left the flowers."

"Okay." I peer over Jake's shoulder as he finds the correct place on the footage and hits the play button. I can feel the tension pulsate around us as we watch avidly to see who is going to appear on the camera. After ten minutes, Jake pulls me onto his lap and wraps his arms around me. I take comfort from him and hope to god that we don't have another Caitlin type scenario on our hands. I know that I am probably overreacting, but being stabbed has made me warier, as it probably would most people. Another five minutes go by of watching nothing, but then the office door opens and I sit forward to get closer to the computer. Jake does the same and we watch, in silence, as someone in a black hoody walks into the room with the flowers. The person keeps their head down the whole time. It definitely looks like a man from the build of the person and from the baggy jeans and trainers.

"Who is that?" I whisper as the person places the flowers on the desk and then they leave the room just as quickly as they entered it.

"I don't know, but I intend to find out," Jake says. He gently lifts me off of his lap so that I am standing, and then he gets to work looking at all of the other cameras in the building.

"I'll go and get us a drink," I say, knowing that Jake will be reluctant to leave my office until he has found answers. I return to the main room and go behind the bar to pour Jake and I a drink. I also make another drink for Martin, but there is no sign of him. I leave it behind the bar and I tell Susie to let Martin know that I am in my office when he returns. I quickly check in with Bonnie but she waves me away and says that she is doing fine. The Den is busy but the three of them can handle it for now. I return to the office, drinks in hand, and give Jake his as he keeps his gaze fixed on the computer screen.

"Any luck?" I ask him.

"I've traced the person through the whole building, but I am yet to be able to see their face clearly. Whoever this is, knows where each and every camera Is. They don't want to be caught."

"Great," I say, sarcastically. I can't believe that yet another person is trying to mess with us. I feel anger build inside of me. *Why can't we just be left alone?*

"I will find out who this is," Jake says, taking my hand in his and squeezing gently.

"Even if you do, when will this end?" I say, exasperated by it all. Jake frowns at me and I quickly explain my outburst. "Why are there so many people willing to interfere in our lives Jake? I'm so fed up of fighting. I don't want to fight anymore." Jake stands up and pulls me into his arms, holding me close to his chest. I wrap my arms around his waist and close my eyes. I may not want to fight, but I will. I would fight with everything that I have for our relationship. It is at this moment that I remember the note that was left on my car.

"Oh my god, the note," I say out loud, causing Jake to loosen his grip on me a little.

"What note?" he asks.

"There was a note left on my car the other day. I presumed it was you that had left it."

"When was this?"

"When I went to Lydia's the other morning. I came out of her flat and the note was on the windshield. It just said, 'missing you already,' so I thought that maybe you had driven past and put it there. I forgot to mention anything as it has been so busy around here."

"Where is the note now?"

"Still in my car." I see Jake's jaw begin to tick. My office door bursts open, startling me, and Martin walks in.

"There you two are. God, a man goes for one little dance and the two of you bugger off like he never existed," Martin says, waltzing in and taking a seat on the sofa.

"Sorry Mart," I say, breaking away from Jake and going over to Martin and sitting beside him.

"It's okay. I actually found a rather nice young man to talk to."

"Oh yeah?" I say and Martin starts giggling like a love-struck teenager. "Well, why don't we get out there and show him how to party?"

"Yes!" Martin says, jumping up from the sofa. I look to Jake as I stand up and he gives a slight nod of his head towards the computer signalling that he will be staying in here, and probably keeping an eye on me in the process. "Come on baby girl. Let's go and booty shake," Martin screeches as he grabs my hand and pulls me out of my office. We hit the dancefloor and start to move in rhythm to the music. Tonight should have just been about having fun, but instead, I now need to find out who has been leaving stuff for me, and why. I thought I was done with being followed, but obviously not. Martin and I dance through a couple more songs and then I leave him to go and get us some more drinks. I need to try and distract my racing mind and not give Martin any cause to worry that I am acting differently. So far, I seem to be doing a good job of that. As I approach the bar, I see that Bonnie is serving a guy, who has his back to me, and she looks all dopey eyed. I stand beside the guy and when I look to see his face, I see that it is Brad. He hasn't noticed me yet as he is too busy gazing at Bonnie. I smile and lean closer so that he will be able to hear me speak.

"You're not distracting my new staff member are you Brad?" I ask him, making him jump. He turns to face me and smiles.

"Not at all. I'm just checking that this young lady isn't being hassled by any men," he replies. I raise an eyebrow at him.

"Right, you mean besides being hassled by you of course?"

"Hey, I am a gentleman. I don't hassle, I just charm."

"Uh huh." I notice that Bonnie is looking from me to Brad and I inform her that Brad is Jake's brother.

"Wow. Good looks really do run in the family huh?" Bonnie says. I'm guessing that she didn't mean to say that out loud, seeing as her hand is now clamped over her mouth.

"I guess so," I say, grinning at her faux pas. She quickly scurries away, her face red with embarrassment.

"Ah Stace, I was making good head way until you came along." He says it in a joking manner and then pouts at me, making me laugh.

"Don't blame me if your techniques aren't having the desired effect. Maybe you should up your game."

"Hmmm. Maybe I already have." The way he speaks and stares at me, makes me feel like he is talking about something else. I don't know what, but his answer definitely has a double meaning. Luckily for me, Martin comes bounding over and puts his arm round my shoulders.

"Where are those drinks baby girl," he asks impatiently. His eyes wander to Brad and he starts to grin. "Oh well, if this is why you are taking so long then, please, take all the time in the world." I roll my eyes at him and Brad's smile suddenly drops from his face.

"I'll just go behind the bar and get our drinks myself. Brad, do you want another?" I ask him.

"Yes please," he says, gulping back the rest of his beer. I chuckle as I make my way behind the bar and busy myself getting the drinks ready. I only have a diet coke as I need to keep a clear head just in case I need to serve on the bar at some point. If that Tom guy had bothered to show up, then I wouldn't have had to worry at all. I decide here and now, that Tom is a lost cause. If he hasn't showed up for his first shift on time, then he clearly doesn't want the job that much. I sigh as I take Brad and Martin their drinks. I will probably end up having to select one of the other, not so great, candidates that I interviewed the other day. I groan at the thought. I pick up my drink, and tell the guys that I am going to my office to check on Jake. Brad decides to follow me, but Martin returns to the dancefloor. I open my office door and Brad follows me inside. Jake looks up from the computer screen and I see his face harden slightly when he sees Brad emerge from behind me.

"Hey bro," Brad says, taking the seat opposite Jake, on the other side of my desk.

"You showed up then," Jake says, his jaw ticking with annoyance.

"Of course I showed up. Didn't you think that I would?" Brad asks, a smirk crossing his face. I walk around to stand by Jake and to take a quick look at the computer screen to see if he has found any clearer images. Jake doesn't answer Brad and instead turns his attention back to the computer. "What are you guys doing anyway?"

"Oh, we're just….."

"Checking some accounts," Jake says, interrupting me. I give him a quizzical look and the look in his eyes tells me that he doesn't want Brad to know what we are looking for. I close my mouth and take the silent hint that he is giving me.

"Seriously? On a Saturday night?"

"Yes Brad. It's part of running your own business," Jake replies.

"Jeez, it's the weekend man, leave work alone for one night." Brad rolls his eyes and I start to feel a little bit awkward at the uneasy words between the two brothers. "Nice flowers," Brad remarks, his eyes settling on the large bouquet that sits on the floor, beside my desk. I tense at his words and I place my hand on Jake's arm to steady myself.

"Uh huh," is all I can think to say.

"What's he done this time to buy you a bouquet like that?" Brad says, nodding his head towards Jake but keeping his eyes fixed on me for an answer. I immediately try to rack my brains for a suitable answer to cover up the fact that they have been left by some creep.

"They're not from me," Jake says, startling me.

"Wow, you got some competition then bro," Brad says, chuckling away at his own comment.

"They're from a supplier who won't take no for an answer," I say, pleased with myself that I have thought of something to say.

"You wanna keep an eye on that supplier Jake," Brad says with a wink.

"He doesn't need to worry," I say, putting my arms around Jake. I lean down and put my cheek next to his. "I'm not going anywhere." I place a kiss on Jake's cheek and I feel some of the tension leave his body from my touch and my words.

"Uh, I think I'm gonna head back to the bar and get another drink. Are you two coming?" Brad asks as he stands up.

"Be there in a minute," Jake says as he fixes his eyes on mine. I hear Brad sigh and then turn to leave my office. When I hear the door click closed, I move my head forward and lock my lips with Jake's.

"Do you know how much I love you?" Jake says when we break apart.

"Hmmm, you may have mentioned it once or twice." I love that he has no hang ups about telling me what I mean to him. "Come on," I say, grabbing his hand. "Let's go and have some fun. We can worry about the flowers tomorrow." I expect him to argue with me, but he doesn't. I just want to have a good time, enjoy myself and forget about whoever it was in my office. The problem will still be there tomorrow, and I have no doubt that Jake will be doing everything that he can to find out who the culprit is.

Chapter Thirty-One.

Stacey.

It's been a couple of days since the offending flowers were delivered to my office. Jake has been scouring the camera footage morning, noon and night. I finally took the laptop off of him last night and hid it from him. He's driving himself crazy trying to figure out who it was that sent them, and the note that was left on my car. He has upped the security at The Den, and I swear that he is watching the cameras each and every time that I am here. I am currently sat in my office and I know that he will be sat at his desk, watching me. It doesn't creep me out that he does this as I know that he is just worried about my safety. I know that after what happened with Caitlin, it frightens him that there is some other loon out to get me. I have tried to reassure him that the security guys wouldn't let anything happen to me, but if watching the cameras gives him peace of mind, then I'm not going to argue with him. I am typing up the rota for next week when there is a knock on my office door.

"Come in," I shout out, looking up from the computer screen. Bonnie appears from behind the door and walks over to my desk. "Everything okay Bonnie?"

"I guess so," she says as she takes a seat and lets out a loud sigh.

"Uh huh. Out with it." I know that something is bugging her. She's usually so upbeat so I am not used to seeing her looking so fed up.

"I feel a bit silly saying this out loud, but........... I can't get him out of my head Stace."

"Who?"

"Brad." She sighs again, but this time she has a dreamy look on her face. "He's got the most mesmerising eyes that I have ever seen." I smile at her. I can definitely agree with her that the Water's family gene for eye colour is strong. Jake's striking eyes were what first attracted me to him.

"Continue," I prompt her, knowing that there is probably more that she wants to say.

"I just can't stop thinking about him. I feel like I am going crazy. Maybe I am crazy? No guy has ever made me think about them like this before. He just...... he oozes sex appeal and masculinity. You know what I mean?" she finishes, looking at me for answers.

"Well, I can understand the way that you are feeling. What you are experiencing right now is similar to what I felt about Jake. Hell, I still feel that way about Jake." Now I am probably the one looking all dreamy eyed. I shake my head to snap myself out of my daze. "Maybe you could ask Brad out for a drink?"

"I can't ask him out!" Bonnie exclaims.

"Why not?" I laugh.

"Because, he is way out of my league Stace."

"Don't be ridiculous," I scold her. "What is it with my friends and putting themselves down?" I don't expect her to answer that, I am just venting out loud. "Listen, I can have a word with him if you like?" Bonnie's eyes widen at my suggestion and I quickly try to put her mind at ease. "I would be subtle, I promise." Before she can answer me however, there is another knock on my office door, and the man in question comes breezing into my office.

"Shit," Bonnie whispers as her head whips round and clocks Brad walking towards my desk.

"Well, well, if it isn't the beautiful Bonnie," Brad says, working his charm. Bonnie blushes and giggles like a school girl.

"That will be all Bonnie. You can go back to the main room now," I say, dismissing her. She nods her head and scrambles to her feet. I watch her as she casually tries to saunter out of the room, but the slight shake in her knees is a dead giveaway that she is putting on a front.

"Good to see you again," Brad says, sitting in the chair that Bonnie has just vacated.

"You too," Bonnie replies. I roll my eyes and cringe slightly at the way her voice sounds all breathless. *Bloody hell, is that what I sound like when I am around Jake? I'd like to think that I have a little bit more sass than that.* Bonnie eventually leaves the office, shutting the door behind her. I turn my attention to Brad as I wonder why on earth he is sitting in my office.

"So, what brings you here?" I ask, knowing that Jake won't be too pleased if he is watching the cameras.

"I just thought that I would come and see my favourite sis-in-law." *Sis-in-law? What is he talking about?* He obviously notices the shock on my face from his comment and he smirks. "Calm down, only joking. Although, you practically are. Jake has never been serious about anyone else."

"Why are you really here Brad?" He seems to be side-stepping whatever it is that he came to say. I may sound blunt, but I just want him to get to the point.

"What, no offer of a drink first?" he asks, putting his arms out either side of him in astonishment.

"You have just walked by the bar. You could have gotten yourself a drink then." Brad starts to laugh although I don't really see why.

"I can see why my brother loves you Stacey. You are one special lady. I just hope that he realises how lucky he is to have you." His words leave me shocked.

"Uh, thanks," I say, awkwardly.

"Relax. I don't mean anything by it. I'm just pleased for Jake, that's all." I know that Brad is speaking, but I fail to see any sincerity in his face. It's almost like the words have been rehearsed. I start to feel uneasy.

"So, you came down here, just to tell me how lucky you think Jake is?"

"No," Brad clears his throat and shifts in the chair. He brings his left leg up and crosses it over his right leg. This may be a perfectly normal action, but it makes my blood run cold. The reason being that, his shoes look just like the ones that the flower guy had on. I should know, Jake blew the images up and has looked at them countless times. "I came to see what you really thought of the flowers now that Jake isn't here." My eyes fly up to his face, and my mouth drops open.

"What?" I say in a small voice.

"I asked you what you really thought of the flowers that I left for you."

"That was you?"

"Yes. Although, I did have some help." I stare at him, flabbergasted. He decides to take my shocked state as a sign to continue talking. "I know that this place is fitted with cameras, so, I needed someone to scope the place out for me properly. Did you not wonder why Tom never showed up?"

"You and Tom?"

"Yes Stacey. Me and Tom. You see, I needed to get an idea of where all of the cameras were so that I could hide my face. I also know that it is only a matter of time before Jake finds out that it was me who sent you the flowers, and of course the note that I left on your car. I knew that he would want to know who sent them, but I didn't expect him to go all FBI on my ass."

"But, why?"

"I like you. Simple." He says it without a care in the world. I don't know what planet that he thinks he is living on, but once Jake finds out, I am certain that he is going to brought back down to earth with a bump.

"But, you don't have to buy flowers, or leave notes for someone, just because you like them." I am trying to think of an appropriate reason for him doing this, but nothing is coming to me.

"When they have a connection, like we do, then people send flowers." He speaks with such confidence that I almost want to laugh at him. *He can't be serious right now.*

"What connection?" At this point, he stands and comes around the desk. I shift back in my seat, feeling more than a little uncomfortable. He perches on the edge of my desk, facing me, and smiles.

"You must feel it Stace. Don't deny it. Since the first day I met you, there has been something. In my doctor's office, you wanted me. I know that you did." My heart rate accelerates, but not in a good way. I have been trapped in an office before, and, right now, I feel on edge. I don't like it, and I need to diffuse whatever the hell is going on. My brain spins as I process the amount of people who have tried to screw Jake and I over. My eyes stare at the floor, and Brad takes this as his opportunity to take hold of my hand. I try to pull it out of his grasp, but his grip is firm.

"Brad, I have no idea what you are talking about. What I do know though is that you need to let go of my hand," I say as I try to free myself from his grasp. He doesn't listen. He holds on tighter. I pray that Jake isn't witnessing this. If he is, then he is going to be going mental. My office phone starts to ring and I peek around Brad at it. I desperately want to answer it. I go to move, but Brad blocks my way.

"You can't dismiss me Stacey." He places my hand over his heart and it is beating wildly.

"Please let go of my hand."

"No. I need you to admit what you feel for me. I need to hear you say that you want me."

"But I don't want you. I love Jake!" I screech at him, my patience running thin.

"I'm not saying that you don't, but you can want me at the same time." His eyes plead with me to give him the answer that he wants, but I can't.

"I'm sorry Brad," I say with a shake of my head. "I just don't feel that way about you."

"Yes you do."

"No, I don't!" I close my eyes in frustration and Brad finally let's go of my hand. My eyes snap open and I hold my hands to my chest so that he can't grab one of them again. "You need to stop this Brad. If Jake finds out about this, then he is never going to speak to you again."

"I don't care," he replies with a shrug of his shoulders.

"You don't care? You don't care?" I shout, my anger rising to the surface. "If you don't care then why the fuck did you come back?" I am on my feet now. Rage courses through me.

"To screw with him. I came back to screw with Jake." My next move shocks Brad and myself, as my hand flies out and slaps him, hard, across the face. His head turns from the force of my slap, and it is at this moment that I see that Jake has entered my office.

Chapter Thirty-Two.

Jake.

Two seconds ago, I had a smile on my face. Two seconds ago, all I wanted to do was have a quiet drink whilst I surprised my girlfriend with a visit to her office. Two seconds ago, all I wanted to do was relax. That is clearly not going to be the case, as I have just walked into Stacey's office to the sight of her smacking Brad around the face. Shock doesn't even come close to what I am feeling right now.

"What's going on?" I say, finding my voice. I close the office door and step closer to Stacey's desk. Her eyes are wide. I keep my gaze fixed on her, ignoring Brad, who is rubbing his cheek.

"She's fucking crazy," Brad says, his answer instantly pissing me off. I clench my fists at my sides and turn to look at him.

"Don't talk about her like that."

"Fucking hell, she really has done a number on you hasn't she?" Brad's cocky nature shines through. He moves around her desk and away from her.

"You bastard," Stacey says, her words directed at Brad.

"Me? You're the one who just tried to hit on me," Brad says. My pulse quickens and I have no doubt in my mind that he is lying. "You clearly don't know her very well bro. You wanna get rid of her before she fucks you over." With that, Stacey rounds her desk and is walking towards Brad, but I catch hold of her arm, halting her in her tracks. She looks at me, her eyes pleading.

"He's lying Jake."

"I know," I whisper to her, not doubting her for a second. I say the words quietly so that Brad can't hear me answer her. I can feel her body trembling with rage, and all I want to do is take her in my arms and make her feel better, but I can't do that right now. I need to deal with Brad first. I move her so that she is stood behind me, effectively making my body a shield between the two of them. I face Brad and stare at him intently.

"It would be a really good idea for you to tell the truth right now." I fold my arms across my chest and I try to push down the anger that I am feeling. I need to hear his explanation and see if he is going to spout a load of bullshit at me.

"I came in here to see if she wanted a drink, and that is when she made a pass at me."

"What?!" Stacey screeches behind me. I move my hand back and take her hand in mine. I squeeze gently to let her know that I am not buying his story.

"She grabbed hold of my hand and started going on about how we had a special connection. When I turned her down, she slapped me and that is when you walked in." He shrugs his shoulders as if this is a normal, everyday occurrence for him. For all I know, it is, but I will be damned if he is going to try and wreck what Stacey and I have together. I can feel the tension pouring off of Stacey behind me. Her breathing is loud and I know that it must be taking all of her willpower to keep quiet. "You have to believe me bro." I actually want to laugh at him at this point, but I don't. I turn my body so that I am looking at Stacey.

"Would you like to tell me what really happened now?" I say to her. Stacey starts to speak, and each time Brad tries to interrupt, I tell him to shut up. I heard his pathetic version, now I want to hear the truth. When she has finished, I simply place a kiss on her hand and then I turn back to Brad.

"You're not going to believe the crap that just came out of her mouth are you?" he asks, and I can see that he is starting to look worried. He knows that I believe her. He knows that I know that he is lying. I am quite proud of myself for not flying across the room and punching him in the face. I let the tension simmer for a few minutes as I watch Brad start to squirm. If I'm not mistaken, I can see beads of sweat forming on his brow. *Good. Let the fucker panic. I should never have agreed to let him back in my life. I know what he is, and I now know that he will never change. He came back here to fuck with me.*

"Let me give you a piece of advice Brad." I say the words slowly so that they sink in. He stares at me, waiting. "Run."

"Run?" he almost looks like he doesn't understand what I am saying.

“Yes. Run. Get the fuck out of here before I really lose my shit.”

“Oh my god. You are actually going to take her word over mine?” he says as he points at Stacey. “Clearly a good fuck is more important than family.” Before I know what I am doing, I am across the room and have Brad pinned against the wall. Not losing my shit didn’t last long. “Jake bro, calm down.”

“Calm down? Fucking calm down?” I shout in his face. “You expect me to be calm when you talk about Stacey like that?”

“She’s just some woman.” I tighten my hold on him, making it clear that his words were the wrong ones.

“Jake,” Stacey’s voice says softly from behind me. “Jake, let him go. He’s not worth it.” Stacey knows what I am capable of when it comes to her. She saw me beat the shit out of Donnie when he attacked her. She will know that I have no qualms about doing the same thing to my brother if he continues to be disrespectful about her. “Please Jake.” Her pleading voice is the only thing that makes me let go of him. If it was anyone else trying to talk me down, then it wouldn’t make a difference. Brad sags against the wall as I step back from him slightly.

“Get out,” I say, my voice low and menacing.

“So that’s it? You want me gone?” Brad says, his arms held out either side of him.

“Yeah. I want you gone.” I have never said these words to him before. I have been pissed off with Brad many times in my life, but I have never actually told him to go.

"You're gonna regret this you know. She won't be around for you forever. I was just trying to show you what a tart she really is." I feel Stacey's hands clamp around my arm to stop me from doing anything. I clench my jaw and try to take a few deep breaths to calm myself down a little.

"This has nothing to do with Stacey. This is about you wanting to screw me over as much as possible."

"Damn straight I want to screw you over," Brad shouts, his true colours shining through. "Why did you get to be the one with the great fucking business? Why did you always get the girls running after you? What makes you so fucking special? I always got glanced over. I was always the one on the side-lines, watching everyone fall over their feet to speak to you. What was wrong with me? Why did you get all the glory?" Brad's 'nice guy' act has well and truly left the building. "I never thought the day would come where Jake fucking Waters would have someone that he cherished more than his own life. When I came back here, I already knew that you had fallen hard for Stacey. It's amazing what you can find out if you know the right people to contact. I must thank Caitlin for all of the information that she gave me about the two of you." I hear Stacey gasp, and even I am a little shocked by his admission of speaking to Caitlin.

"You spoke to Caitlin?" Stacey says from behind me.

"Oh yeah. She was more than willing to help me try and split you two up. It was her idea to leave the note on your car and the flowers in your office. She thought it would be a nice touch, seeing as she stalked you for weeks before she stabbed you."

"You sick, twisted......."

"Yeah, yeah. Call me what you like, but you can't deny that it was a good fucking plan," Brad says, cutting Stacey off mid-sentence. "It's just a shame that it hasn't ended in the way that Caitlin and I had hoped."

"And what was the end game?" I ask, almost wishing that I hadn't voiced my curiosity.

"To gain your trust and leave you heartbroken bro. To make you feel worthless, like I have done all of these years." I scoff at his, and Caitlin's, ridiculous plan. Is this the best that they could come up with? They clearly underestimated mine and Stacey's commitment to one another.

"Brad?" Stacey says from behind me, making me turn around to look at her. Her eyes are wide and she has gone pale.

"Yes Stacey?" Brad replies.

"That morning that you came to the house to invite me to breakfast, how did you get in?" I turn away from Stacey to look at Brad as it finally clicks into place for me that she didn't actually let him in the house on the morning in question.

"I was wondering when you were going to ask about that," Brad replies, a smirk crossing his face. "During my time of plotting with Caitlin, she divulged the information that she had hidden a key to the house." I hear Stacey gasp again and my hands ball into fists at his answer. "You see, when Jake and Caitlin were fucking one another, she had the sense to borrow Jake's key and make a copy." I clench my jaw as the anger within me starts to boil over. "Jake never knew about the key that she had copied, obviously. She hid the key in a safe place, just in case she ever needed to use it."

"Oh my god," Stacey says in a whisper.

"Thanks to Jake's carelessness, before you came along," Brad says directing his comment to Stacey, "he gave Caitlin the opportunity to have access to his house keys."

"I feel sick," Stacey says.

"You need to leave Brad," I say, needing him to get as far away from me as possible before I wrench my arm out of Stacey's grasp and I launch myself at him.

"And what are you going to do about it if I don't?" he says, cockiness taking over. He is going to regret asking me that question.

"If you stay around here, then I will ruin you. I will have you discredited as a doctor, and I will make sure that you never work anywhere near here, ever again."

"You don't have the power to do that."

"Don't be so sure Bradley." I only ever use his full name when I mean business. He knows that. He looks at me, warily, clearly assessing his options since his plan has backfired. "I have money, and you and I both know that money talks. I have connections due to my business. I have ways of making your life hell."

"You wouldn't do that."

"If you believe that I wouldn't, then you're more stupid than I thought. The line that you have crossed this time can never be repaired. As far as I am concerned, I have no brother." I can see that my words have stung him, but I couldn't give a fuck. He has never been a brother to me, so it's not really any loss.

"You know, it was fun while it lasted. I would like to say that I regret my actions, but all I regret is the fact that I wasn't able to play this out a bit longer. I reckon another month or two and she would have been putty in my hands," Brad says, pointing at Stacey. I feel Stacey's grip on my arm tighten, so that I don't go over to him and unleash my full fury. I grind my teeth together so hard that I am surprised that I don't chip a tooth. As I look at Brad, with what I am sure is a death stare, he finally shakes his head and turns away from me. He walks to the office door, opening it.

"Brad?" I say, getting his attention before he walks out of my life for good. He looks at me, and I can see the hate filling his eyes. "Don't ever come back."

Chapter Thirty-Three.

Jake.

Stacey flops down onto the sofa in her office after getting us both a drink from the bar. I have watched the footage of what happened before I got here, and I am furious. Watching it has done me no favours whatsoever. Stacey told me not to torture myself by looking at it, but it turns out that I am a glutton for punishment. When his hand grabbed hers, I wanted to hurl the computer across the room. I don't understand how he thought that he was going to get away with lying. The cameras prove what really happened, and he knew that cameras were in here. I don't think that I will ever understand how he thought his plan would work.

"How are you doing?" she asks me, her hand covering mine.

"I've been better," I admit. I'm annoyed at myself more than anything. I'm annoyed that another person came into our lives and tried to destroy what we have.

"I'm sorry about Brad," she says.

"Don't be," I say, pulling her close to me, my arm around her shoulders. She snuggles her head against me and I inhale her scent.

"I really thought that he wanted to be part of your life. I never would have tried to convince you to let him back in if I had known what he was really like. I should have listened to you."

"Hey," I say softly as I use my free hand to lift her chin up so she is looking at me. Her eyes look sad and I want to take away that look more than anything. "Don't you dare go blaming any of this on yourself." I know how her mind works, and I am not prepared to let her think that she had any influence on Brad's intentions.

"But….."

"No buts. He's out of our lives for good. All that matters is that we have each other." I sound like a soppy sod, but I don't care. I need her to know that she is all that I care about. She sighs and takes a sip of her drink.

"We need to get the locks changed at the house," Stacey says.

"Already on it. There will be someone out first thing tomorrow morning."

"Phew. That's one less thing to worry about I suppose."

"I'm also having some security cameras installed outside, just for the time being." I say. I need to make sure that Stacey is safe.

"Do we really need to do that?" Stacey asks. "I mean, Caitlin is in prison and, if Brad has any sense, then he will be gone."

"I'm not taking any chances. They're both screwed in the head." I'm not one hundred percent convinced that

Brad will go, so it is better to be safe than sorry. Stacey lets out a loud sigh.

"Are things ever going to run smoothly for us Jake?" she asks me.

"Sure they will. Whatever we face only makes us stronger. No one is going to break us."

"Promise?"

"Promise," I say as I lean down and place a kiss on the end of her nose. She smiles and rests her head on my shoulder. As I sit here, her body close to mine, I feel thankful that she is willing to stick around and put up with all of the shit that comes from being with me. This woman has been stabbed, stalked, and hit on by my brother, because of me. If she were any lesser woman, she would have run a mile ages ago. I know that she isn't going anywhere. I know that I will do everything in my power to make her happy. I also know that, one day soon, I am going to ask this woman to be my wife.

THE END.

The conclusion of Stacey and Jake's story is coming soon in the final book of the Perfect Series...........

To keep up to date with Lindsey's book news, you can find her via:

Twitter:
@Lindsey_perfect

Facebook:
@lindseypowellperfect

Instagram:
@lindseypowellperfect

She can also be found on Goodreads, and at her Amazon Author page.

Author Acknowledgements.

So, the third book of the Perfect Series, WOW!

I hope that you all enjoyed the third instalment, and

that Jake and Stacey are still capturing your hearts.

Thank you once again to my other half, James, my family

and friends for their support, and my children for their

patience.

A lot of hard work goes into producing these books, and

I am still lucky enough to have my right-hand woman with me

to make everything run smoothly. Vikki, you are just brilliant,

and I look forward to working on my upcoming projects with

you.

With Perfect Disaster finished, I am now working on finalising

everything for the fourth book in the Perfect Series.

I can't wait to share it with you!

Please don't forget to leave me a review on Amazon, or Goodreads,

as each one is so important, especially to an indie author.

To all of my readers, thank you!

Much love as always,

Lindsey.

26192228R00162

Printed in Great Britain
by Amazon